THE PONY PROBLEM

Jean tugged her hat clear to her eyes, crouched down, and kicked the pony. They cantered across the lawn, probably kicking up chunks of grass, along the side of the house, past a swing set and Big Wheel, and through a gap in the poplars to the Wilcoxes' backyard.

Out of nowhere, Mrs. Wilcox sprang up at them, waving a leaf rake.

"Oh, no you don't!" she screamed. "Get out of this yard!"

Hopscotch shied and Jean lost her reins. Thrown off course, too fast to stop, unswerving, they headed for the swimming pool.

Mrs. Wilcox screamed again.

The edge wasn't high, and Hopscotch never hesitated. Neat and clean, with her ears pricked forward, she jumped into the swimming pool and landed with a crashing splash in three feet of water.

Water rose in a great sweeping sheet and soaked Mrs. Wilcox, and Jean fell into the pool. . . .

The
Pony Problem
Barbara Holland

PUFFIN BOOKS

PUFFIN BOOKS
Published by the Penguin Group
Penguin Books USA Inc., 375 Hudson Street, New York, New York 10014, U.S.A.
Penguin Books Ltd, 27 Wrights Lane, London W8 5TZ, England
Penguin Books Australia Ltd, Ringwood, Victoria, Australia
Penguin Books Canada Ltd, 10 Alcorn Avenue, Toronto, Ontario, Canada M4V 3B2
Penguin Books (N.Z.) Ltd, 182–190 Wairau Road, Auckland 10, New Zealand

Penguin Books Ltd, Registered Offices: Harmondsworth, Middlesex, England

First published in the United States of America by E.P. Dutton, 1977
Published in Puffin Books, 1993

1 3 5 7 9 10 8 6 4 2

Library of Congress Catalog Card Number: 92-62886
ISBN 0-14-036339-4

Printed in the United States of America
Set in Aster

For Emily and Dewdrop

1

It all began back when Jean Monroe was six years old, and her mother gave her, for her birthday, a subscription to something called *The Children's Hour, a story-time magazine for little folks*. It was pretty awful, full of stories like "Tommy and the Moon Machine" and "Where Is Curly Chipmunk?" But on the back page, twice a year, there was a contest called "Name This Pony and Win It for Your Very Own."

Entries were judged on the basis of originality, sincerity, and aptness of thought, and the decision of the judges was final.

Jean named the first pony Misty, in crooked first-grade printing, and sent it in.

Nothing happened. She named the second pony Whirlwind. When her birthday came around again she asked her mother to renew the subscription to *The Children's Hour*.

"Are you sure?" said her mother. "I never see you reading it."

Jean was sure. She named the third pony Golden Boy and the fourth Sagebrush, and got her subscription renewed again.

After Candlelight, Shadow, Vanity, Beechnut, Wayover, Pretty Please, and Honey Bee, she was past eleven. You had to be under twelve. This was the last pony.

She and her friend Shelley Wolfram, who lived three doors down, bent over the pony's picture as if the magic name might be written on it, in lemon juice maybe. If you looked closely, or breathed on it long enough, it might mysteriously appear. This one was a chocolate palomino mare with a trailing sweep of flaxen tail and a great ruff of flaxen mane and forelock, out of which she peered alertly.

"It's the prettiest one yet," said Jean. "Look how smart she looks. Look at her soft little nose. I've *got* to win this one."

"You say that every time," said Shelley. "Mother says nobody really wins these things."

"They do too. *Somebody* does. And if somebody can, I can. Fudge Sundae," she added, and wrote it down on her list. "Woolly Bear. Peanut Brittle. Oh, why can't I *think*?" She pounded her fist on her head, further crushing her battered hat.

"It ought to be something about her mane and tail," said Shelley. "All blond like that. What about Movie Star?"

Jean made a face but wrote it down. "It's so hard to name a pony. Look at all the stupid names they have, you can tell it's hard. Sunny and Missy and Lightning and Peanut and Star Boy and Princess. Every single pony in the world's named something like that."

Shelley sighed and looked out the window. "You better pick one pretty soon. You've got to get it postmarked. What about Chocolate Pie?"

"Mm." Jean closed her eyes and pressed her fingers on them. The name existed. It was somewhere. She only had to find it. Touch the tail of it, just for an instant, to feel its

2

shape. It was like straining to see in the dark, or trying to remember a dream. She stared at the blackness inside her eyelids until she began to feel sick, and then opened them and stared at the picture.

"Cinnamon," said Shelley. "Ginger. Nutmeg. Butterscotch."

"Butterscotch. . . ." Jean stared down at the picture, and a faint sound rustled inside her head. "Hopscotch," she said.

"No," said Shelley. "That doesn't have anything to do with ponies. It has to be something that goes with the pony."

"No, it doesn't. Listen. There're only about six things that go with a pony, any pony. Like, if it's dark you can call it Midnight or Shadow, and a sorrel you call Honey or Golden Girl or something. I guess they get thousands of them every time. For a chocolate palomino they'll get a million entries like Chocolate Sundae and Flaxen Miss and things like that. They'll be glad to see Hopscotch. It'll be different."

"It's dumb," said Shelley decisively. "You can't call a pony Hopscotch."

"I can," said Jean. "I'm going to." But already she felt less sure, and pinched her lower lip between her teeth while she printed it out slowly and carefully, in capitals. The rest of the coupon had been filled out a week ago, waiting, and the envelope was addressed and stamped. This was the last time, the last chance. She licked the envelope and pressed it shut with her fist, holding it down hard.

"You better come on," said Shelley. "Suppose you miss the mail collection? It's almost five."

They ran down Maryellen Lane, Jean holding her hat on with one hand and pressing the envelope to her shirt with the other, past all the houses that were exactly the same but different colors, so people could tell them apart, the tan Wilcoxes', the white Reeces', Shelley's green one, the white Seidles', the tan one on the corner of Wisteria Drive where the mailbox was. "Wait *up*," called Shelley, panting.

The envelope dropped into darkness and the mailbox clanged shut, and sounded hollow. Jean pulled the door back open and tried to see in, but it was all black. You couldn't reach in, either, if you changed your mind. She stared at the shiny blue paint. "Hopscotch," she said aloud, testing it. "Hopscotch?" But there was no answer, only Shelley breathing hard. Nothing to tell her if she was right, and weeks and weeks to wait before she knew.

"I don't see how I'm going to stand it, waiting," she said. "I've got a stomachache already."

"I don't," said Shelley. "Let's go back to your house and see if there's anything to eat."

"But Shell, it's the last time. My last chance."

"Thank goodness," said Shelley placidly. "It's an awful fuss. And besides, it isn't as if anyone *else* had a pony."

"Plenty of kids do."

"Not around here," said Shelley.

Jean waited, and the weeks did pass, and then the man came bringing Hopscotch in a battered aluminum trailer, and handed her to Jean, right there on the sidewalk in front of 10007 Maryellen Lane, Dogwood Estates, Bedlington, New Jersey, and Jean held her by the halter and signed the receipt with her left hand, leaning on the fender of the truck and shaking so that no one in the world could have read what she'd written.

The pony and the girl had just barely time to exchange a quick shy glance of recognition, and for Jean to touch the small velveteen nose in greeting, before things started to close in.

4

Doors banged. There were voices, and footsteps, and people calling and running. At first they just seemed surprised, and then they were angry and raised their voices.

"Won it in a contest," Shelley Wolfram said.

"Not in *this* neighborhood, I hope!"

"It's not sanitary."

"This is a residential neighborhood, not some farm."

"Bring down the property values."

"Think of the flies," said Mrs. Pike, and shuddered.

Shelley's mother said mildly, "I'm sure Jean isn't going to keep it *here*."

"But where else could I keep it?" cried Jean. "It's mine."

Mrs. Wilcox next door couldn't have been madder if Jean had won a saber-toothed tiger. She actually called the police, and they came, two of them in a squad car, and were really very nice. They said the area was zoned against keeping pigs, and chickens or geese or anything at all with feathers, but for some reason there was nothing in the regulations about ponies, and unless the pony bit somebody there wasn't anything the police could do.

So they went away, but nobody else did.

More and more people kept coming. It was the most interesting thing to happen in Dogwood Estates since the Bells' kitchen caught fire. All the kids and mothers on Maryellen Lane came to stand around on the sidewalk, the mothers complaining and the kids mostly just staring, and some of the bigger ones bragging about how they could ride her, but backing off hastily when she stamped her foot. Mrs. Reece said it was just the kind of thing you'd expect from the Monroes. Just then Hopscotch dropped a pile of poop, and everyone said, "See? Think of all that filth, and the children tracking it into the house," even though everyone's dog did the same thing all over the sidewalks.

Jean couldn't even go inside and get away from them,

because she had to keep standing there holding the pony by her red halter. There was nothing else to do. She wanted her mother badly. Even her brother would do, but he'd gone to see a chess match in Bedlington. There was no one to help.

Mrs. Monroe, alone of all the women on Maryellen Lane, worked. Jean's father had been dead for years, and every day her mother took the train from Bedlington, where all the men stood on the station platform reading their papers and waiting for the 8:22 and she was the only woman, and went in to the science museum, where she classified and took care of the collection of moths and butterflies, in a room full of metal trays and cabinets of them, all stuck down with their Latin names.

Jean and her brother took care of themselves, and the house. They did their best for the house, but the truth is, it rather stuck out on Maryellen Lane for its neglected, shabby look. Paint was peeling off. One of the azalea bushes had died, and stood there reproachfully under the picture window, like a murdered skeleton. The lawn was mostly weeds. And now there was a pony on it, and a pile of poop, and all the angry people.

Hopscotch fidgeted and laid her small ears back and rolled her eyes. She hadn't had anything to eat but some weeds from the lawn, and a saucepan full of water Shelley brought her. She backed up, dragging at Jean's arm and trying to pull her halter off over her ears.

"Vicious, too," said Mrs. Reece.

"Stop it," Jean whispered. "Stand still. Please." Tears were leaking over the edges of her eyes, and she kept her back to the neighbors so they wouldn't see. It was hateful, it was unbelievable, to finally get what you'd always wanted most in the world, and have people spoil it.

6

"All we have to do," said Mrs. Seidle, "is get the zoning ordinance changed."

"That takes too long," snapped Mrs. Wilcox. "We'd better think of something faster."

Mrs. Pike said, "I read somewhere where people can catch hoof-and-mouth disease from horses."

And then Mrs. Monroe came home, along with the fathers, all the cars pulling into their different driveways and everyone getting out with newspapers in their hands and coming over to see what was happening.

Mrs. Monroe, of course, was just as surprised as everyone else. Also, Hopscotch stepped on her foot. But she promised the neighbors that she'd take care of everything, that naturally she'd never expected Jean to win a pony, that of course she couldn't keep it there on Maryellen Lane, that they'd make arrangements to get rid of it as soon as they could.

By this time, the women all had to go home anyway and make supper, and the men were too tired to care. Except Mr. Wilcox, who said he'd give them a week and then he'd handle the matter himself.

Mrs. Monroe found some clothesline, left from the time the dryer broke, and they tied Hopscotch to a dogwood tree. For dinner they gave her what was left of the Sugar Smacks and a whole box of Corn Flakes, and four more saucepans full of water. Jean fell asleep in a chair.

The clothesline was plastic, and it stretched and broke.

In the morning, Hopscotch was in the Reeces' backyard, where the grass was better, and on her way she had pooped in the Wilcoxes'. Jean cleaned it up, apologizing furiously over and over. The Reeces' baby had never seen a pony before, and it was screaming its head off.

The Monroes didn't have any carrots, so Jean grabbed a

handful of parsley and went to catch Hopscotch, coaxing and scolding and waving the parsley at her and diving for the halter. Both of them went through a flower bed and mashed a lot of petunias.

Jean took all her money out of the bank. She had been saving it since she was eight years old and beginning to wonder if maybe she wouldn't win a pony after all, and would have to buy one.

She bought six rolls of clothesline. She and Shelley wrapped it around the three dogwood trees and the little white birch in the front yard to make a fence. While they were eating lunch, Hopscotch crawled out from under and went clear down to Wisteria Drive, where they finally found her eating the grass around a fire hydrant, surrounded by a crowd of little boys.

Jean bought two more rolls of clothesline. Where the fence was longest and weakest, between two of the dogwoods, they added another support, a pole from Shelley's badminton set.

"It looks like a squirrel's nest on the city dump," said Mrs. Wilcox. "A nice thing to look right out our windows and see. Are you going to get rid of that smelly thing, or are we going to have to take steps?"

With the rest of the money Jean bought hay and a pitchfork and a bucket, a brush and a hoof-pick and a second-hand bridle with the reins broken and knotted together.

"But lamb," said her mother. "You *are* going to have to get rid of it, you know, and you're spending all your money."

"But I might as well be able to ride her while she's here. And I have to *feed* her." Secretly, she refused to believe they would ever have to get rid of her. It was not to be thought of. The fuss was dying down. Maybe people would simply get used to having a pony around, and stop noticing.

She borrowed four dollars from her brother Donald and bought a big sheet of plastic to wrap the hay in, to keep it dry.

"It looks like a slum," said Mrs. Reece, pushing her baby past in its stroller. "When are you going to get rid of it? Can't you sell it or something?" The baby started to scream, and she had to hurry on before Jean could think of an answer.

There wasn't any answer, really. How could you work all your life to win a pony and then have to sell it? She thrust it out of her mind.

When Mr. Reece and Mr. Pike from across the street had both come over to talk about it, Mrs. Monroe called the S.P.C.A. for advice. They were nice, but they didn't know of any place to keep Hopscotch. They didn't have a place. They kept dogs and cats, and once they'd had a raccoon, but nothing bigger. However, they would come and put the pony "painlessly to sleep" and not charge anything, and they said some nasty things about contests. Mrs. Monroe said she'd keep it in mind.

Then Mr. and Mrs. Wilcox came over and were very rude indeed, and after that her mother made Jean put up a sign saying PONY FOR SALE on the birch tree. Of course nobody driving down Maryellen Lane wanted to buy a pony, but Mrs. Monroe said it looked as though they were trying, anyway.

In the meantime, Jean brushed and combed and rode her pony, and sat for hours in the pen talking to her, sometimes with Shelley, sometimes alone, and fussed with her shaggy forelock and velvety ears, and carried mountains of poop around back to bury.

Mrs. Rimmel, from clear down in the next block, called

9

up one evening to say the flies were driving her crazy and she was going to report it to the Board of Health.

Jean's mother said that every time the phone rang now her hands and feet went icy, and she put an ad in the paper to sell Hopscotch, but the only person who answered it was a man who sounded so businesslike that Jean thought of horsemeat, and told him the pony was already sold.

Now summer was over. School had started again, fall was here, and so was Hopscotch. Still.

2

The school bus left Jean and Shelley off at Wisteria and Tulip, and they walked home together. The houses stepped past them in an orderly row—white, green, white, tan— each with a few young trees in front, looking fragile and weedy, and each with a row of azaleas under the picture window. Some had a tricycle abandoned on the front walk, and some had round blue swimming pools sprouting from their backyards. Sometimes a baby cried.

"I hate it the way they're all alike," said Jean. "It's so *boring*. If they're all just the same, why bother to have so many? You could have just one house, and one family, and make the rest with one of those trick-mirror things."

"It's okay," said Shelley peacefully. "I like it. It's nice when you go to visit somebody, and you know right where everything is, the bathroom and everything. It's like, no matter where you go, you're home."

"Then there's no sense going anywhere, if it's all the same."

"Oh, you're always hating how things are." Shelley stepped around an empty stroller on the sidewalk with a gnawed Fig Newton on its seat, and shifted her books to the other hip. "You just get in trouble trying to change things. Like your hair. Look what happened to that."

Jean pulled her hat down over her ears, as if Shelley might snatch it off. It was a man's hunting-and-fishing kind of hat that had once belonged to her father and was now quite shapeless, with its green-and-brown check faded to mud color. It had a band around the crown where she kept pencils and her library card and sometimes a blue jay's feather. It was making her teacher furious.

"I bet you sleep in it," said Shelley.

"Sure I sleep in it. Suppose the house caught fire, and they put up a ladder and came in the window, and there I'd be?"

"Take it off a sec. I want to see."

"No."

"Boy, was that dumb." Shelley giggled rudely, remembering what was under the hat.

They came to the Wolframs' house first, a green one with the garage part on the left. A small sign on the front lawn said THE WOLFRAMS, and Jean said it looked as if the whole family was buried under there.

They did not go in. Mrs. Wolfram disapproved of eating between meals, so all her children went somewhere else after school.

They went on past the white Reeces' and the tan Wilcoxes' to the white Monroes'.

"Anyway," said Shelley, "you can't say *your* house looks just like everyone else's."

Hopscotch leaned on the top string of her clothesline fence, making the dogwood bend dangerously, and whuffled at the girls. "I'm home, I'm home," cried Jean, and hugged her around the neck.

It was always a great warm wash of relief to come home and find her still here, and still safe. At school, she chewed her nails and brooded and fretted the day away, worrying. It was awful to have to leave her alone here with people who hated her. Anything could happen. She could be poisoned, maybe with just a few drops of something on a sugar cube. Or Jean could come home and just find her gone. The strings untied, and no pony, and no way ever to find out what happened.

She rubbed her cheek against the brown fur cheek and sharp halter buckles, and the pony pulled away to poke her nose at Jean's pockets. "I haven't got your carrot yet, piggy, wait a minute. Her bucket's empty, Shell, turn on the hose, will you? *Ouch,* stop pushing me! Isn't she beautiful? How can people be so stupid and awful?"

Hopscotch was indeed a picture-book pony, and her tail, brushed with Jean's own hairbrush, touched the ground. Out of the mop of straw-colored forelock her small pointy ears poked up with interest, and she watched the girls from under eyelashes that were blond against her dappled-brown face.

"I wish you wouldn't make so many poops," said Jean lovingly. "It took me all day to dig that new hole around back, and it's almost full already. Couldn't you just *stop* for a while?"

Hopscotch tossed her head, and bent down to rub a fly off her face along one delicate foreleg. Jean threw her a section of hay, and Shelley filled the bucket, and they went inside.

"There's no jelly," said Jean. "I'll make them with cream cheese."

"Peanut butter and *cream cheese* sandwiches?" said Shelley. But she ate one anyway, opening its edge from time

13

to time to inspect the contents. Jean went upstairs to change.

Her brother Donald was in his room, as usual, his neat bare room with no posters on the walls, and he had, as usual, made his bed before he went to school. He left before Jean in the morning, on the high school bus, and came home first.

His chess pieces were set out on the little chess table, and he sat hunched over them, his back curved, his chin in his left hand, his left elbow on his right wrist, the way he always sat. He stared down at the chessboard as if he expected the pieces to slide around checkmating each other. Whenever Jean thought of Donald, which wasn't actually very often, she saw him sitting like that, waiting, listening for a message, a signal, from the gods of chess.

His other occupation was math. There were only eight books on his bookshelf, all neatly standing straight, but each book was years of work to go through, all written in symbols Jean couldn't imagine understanding, ever. Once she had asked him to help her with a math problem, and he was horrified. *"That,"* he had said, "is not mathematics. *That* is arithmetic." He sounded as if arithmetic was a kind of disease, and he wouldn't help.

"Hello," he said, without looking up. "I think your pony's out of water."

"You might have gotten her some. The hose's right there."

"Mm. Yes, I guess I could have. I didn't think of it."

"Boy, I'd hate to belong to you."

Donald unfolded himself and stood up and, still without looking at Jean in his doorway, moved around to the other side of the chess table where another chair sat waiting for him, and slunched down into it to inspect the chessboard from that side. There were hardly any pieces left on it, just the kings and a queen, a bishop, three knights and a rook and a scatter of pawns. "Never despise your pawns," he used to tell her, as she flung them away on reckless, suicidal moves. He hardly ever played with her anymore, though. He said she had reached the limits of her capacity for abstract thought.

In her own untidy room, Jean fed the gerbils and changed into her riding pants. Even in the dark, you could tell they were her riding pants; they hadn't been washed for a long time, and almost stood up by themselves. They smelled more like Hopscotch than Hopscotch herself. Pulling off her school shirt, she kept her hat tightly on her head with one hand, wiggling and squirming herself out and into her old sweater.

Once a week, Jean took that hat off to wash her hair, quickly, with the bathroom door locked. Then she pulled it back on again to sit in the cooling water turning the taps with her toes and reading, cold trickles from the secret mess inside oozing out from under the hat brim and down her neck.

Downstairs, Shelley was eating some potato chips she had found.

"You coming to ride?" asked Jean.

"These are soggy. No, I guess not. Mom wants me to clean up my room, and go shopping with her, and stuff."

Jean listened to a very short twang of envy run through her. That was what mothers, real mothers, did. That was how a real house ran. You had to clean up your room, go shopping, wash your hands, all at a special time, and the house ticked along like a watch, turning and turning through the hours, always the same. Very briefly, she thought it would be cozy to live like that, and then she thought it would be dull, and went to get a carrot from the refrigerator.

3

Hopscotch pushed anxiously at the fence, making it harder to untie. The gate part was four strands of plastic clothesline tied to the larger dogwood tree, which was showing signs of exhaustion, and each strand had to be untied, every time. Jean's fingernails were always broken off short.

She bridled the pony and stood back a little, cried "Hup!" and swung herself up onto the warm round back and almost over onto her head on the other side. Not owning a saddle was good exercise.

Happy to be out, Hopscotch broke into a trot before Jean was settled, and had to be hauled in.

There was no use hurrying, anyway. The workmen on the new houses didn't leave until 4:15, and Jean didn't like getting there sooner. Once in the summer she'd arrived early, and someone turned on the big circular saw and sliced a board with a screaming, shrieking whine like all the horse-nightmares on earth, and Hopscotch simply flew into a million pieces. By the time Jean had picked herself up and looked around, the pony was halfway to Bedlington, and too jittery to be caught for hours.

16

Clop, clop, clippy, along the sidewalk. There was no place in Dogwood Estates to ride, no place a pony was allowed to be. On the sidewalk, mothers wanted to push strollers and baby carriages, with a kid on a Big Wheel trailing along behind. In the street, cars and delivery trucks blew their horns, hard. The grassy strip between was narrow and dotted with fire hydrants, and besides, the people who lived in the houses along it felt it belonged to them. They were the ones who had to mow it. On Tuesday and Saturday they blocked it up with trash cans. In wet weather, Hopscotch left footprints. Once in a while she left something more. The Wilcoxes, the Seidles, and down beyond Wisteria the Bells and the Rimmels often raised their windows to holler at Jean, and she pulled her hat down tightly and kept looking straight ahead.

Clup-clup. Clup-clup. The rocking rhythm of horse-walking soothed her, and her problem filled her head and took over.

What to do with Hopscotch. How to keep a pony when you couldn't keep a pony. There must be a way. But suppose there wasn't?

Suppose everything failed, and her mother had to call the S.P.C.A. again, and they came and gave her a shot, and her bright dark eyes filmed over and her front legs buckled, and she folded up on the bare trampled ground of her pen, struggled for a minute, and then flattened out, with her neck and head stretched in the dirt and her long brushed tail tangled in a mess, and they knotted ropes around her delicate quick legs and hauled her away in a truck? Watching it drive away, you would see only the bunched-up little hoofs, no bigger than teacups, that would never go anywhere again. Nothing left but trash, to be hauled off and dropped in a pit somewhere.

All because Jean won her in a contest. Jean, and not some other kid with a stable and fields and fences.

Jean thought about all this but did not believe. It was almost a deliciously horrible thing to let herself think about, like ghost stories, because it could never come true. There was a way to keep Hopscotch. All she had to do was find it.

They clopped across Wisteria, and turned toward the hill.

Two boys on bikes came swooping by, showing off, leaning back no-hands. "Funny-looking car you've got there!"

"What kind of gas does it run on?"

Sometimes the kids were just as dumb as the grown-ups, thinking a pony was funny just because nobody else had one. You'd think they'd be happy to see something different for a change.

"How many gears does it have?" They swooped away laughing, steering by throwing their weight from side to side, swinging in close to the curb and then swaying across to the other curb. Hopscotch ignored them. Her ears were pricked toward the top of the hill where the new houses were being built.

If only there was a place where Jean could hide her. But you couldn't hide anything that big on Dogwood Estates. If only they could run away together, with some extra clothes and a hoof-pick on Jean's back in a schoolbag, and live in the woods. What woods? Eat acorns? And winter coming?

If she could earn some money, maybe she could find a stable somewhere, and board her. Huh. Sixty or seventy or maybe more dollars a month.

Hide her in the house somehow, and tell the neighbors she was gone.

Poison the neighbors. No, new neighbors would come, there would always be neighbors.

There had to be a way.

Jean was a person who believed faithfully, fervently, the way some people believe in rainbows or first stars, that she could do anything. Anything at all. She could win a pony in a contest. She could find a way to keep her. She could, if she happened to want to do such a weird thing, get to the moon or make all A's on her report card, or understand her brother's books, or change herself into a toadstool. You only had to want to, and keep at it.

And so she thought, as she rolled gently to the pony's walk, up Tulip Drive, and her eyes were fixed on nothing. Her mind kept picking and picking at the problem, the way a prisoner in a dark place might keep picking at the wall with his fingers, feeling over every inch of the smoothness for a loose place or a little break in the plaster.

There had to be a way.

Halfway up the hill, the sidewalk stopped. From here on up, it looked like the end of the world, but it was freedom for Hopscotch.

At least for a few more weeks. Dogwood Estates was stretching and growing and reaching on up the hill and, for all Jean knew, on across the county, and the state, and maybe the whole world. Some of the new houses were almost finished. Some of them, farther up, were still just frameworks of board, and on beyond, they were only concrete-block foundations waiting for a house to grow on them. At the very top of the hill, land was still being cleared. Bulldozers had pushed the scraggly trees into piles to be burned. One pile was burning already, and sent a long slow curtain of smoke down over the rest of Dogwood Estates.

It looked like a school filmstrip on how to build houses, only in reverse, with the finished ones first and the bulldozers last. How to unbuild houses.

Hopscotch stopped. They usually stopped here, and

looked back down at the lived-in part of Dogwood Estates.

Shelley always said it looked like a game. She said she'd love to give it to her twin brothers for Christmas, with little toy cars to push down the streets, and little wooden people to push in and out of the houses.

Jean thought the only really nice thing about it was the television aerials. They hovered over each house like a square of spiderweb, and gave it all a nice floaty, lacy look.

A burst of little boys came out of the end of a sewer pipe and chased each other away, scrambling over mountains of dirt and leaping into foundations. All the kids came up here to play. Down below, the backyard swing sets hung limp and deserted, and the round blue backyard swimming pools reflected the sky.

Someone had moved Jean's sawhorses again. She tied Hopscotch to a steamroller and rearranged them, including the in-and-out.

She had never gotten as far as jumping in camp, but Hopscotch was teaching her now. Sometimes Jean fell off, and sometimes she lost her balance and jerked the pony's mouth, but they worked on it every day and she was getting better all the time. She hardly ever fell clear off anymore. Probably she ought to have a hard hat, she thought. At camp, kids who jumped had to wear them. She wondered how much they cost, and where you could buy one.

The little kids who came up here to play hardly noticed Jean and the pony anymore. They just stayed out of the way, and dug caves and gouged out slides in the piles of dirt, and built things with cinder blocks.

Jean worked Hopscotch over her course, and around the end house where a ditch and a pile of gravel had been added since yesterday. The pony jumped those too, since they were there, and switched her tail and trotted around to the beginning again. There wasn't really room enough to canter.

Some boys had built a lean-to out of boards propped against a foundation wall, and were crawling in and out of it, their knees crusty with mud, pretending it was a house, or a fort.

Jean remembered when she and Shelley used to come up here, last year when it was all just scrubby woods. They always built things too. Houses. Tepees out of small trees tied together at the top, and castles from stones laid together to make walls, and a cave dug laboriously under a fallen tree. Finished, they would sit in them for a while and wonder: How would it feel to live here, to live in a tepee, or a castle, or a cave? It felt important. It gave you someone interesting to be.

Hopscotch refused the in-and-out, suddenly, so that Jean slid up onto her neck and some little girls laughed.

It was time to go home, anyway. Tuesday, with potatoes to peel.

The ride downhill was familiar, the pony knew the way, and Jean's mind was turned loose to worry again. A place to keep a pony. Oh, dear, why wasn't life as simple as it ought to be? Why couldn't you build a castle out of rocks and branches and live in it, or dig a stable under a fallen tree?

Maybe she could buy a piece of land from the builders here, a piece they weren't using, if only she had some money.

Or *find* a piece of land, far away from anywhere, and build something on it without telling anyone. A fence, and a lean-to shelter of sticks, or even steal some bits of lumber nobody wanted. But there wasn't any land far away from anywhere. There were roads all over, houses, shopping centers, the new industrial park down by the train station. Someone wanted everything, and was using it.

She looked down the street for her own house. It wasn't there.

She scowled and stared harder. No yard was strung with clothesline and trampled by pony feet. It ought to be right there in front of her. It wasn't.

It made her feel a little dizzy, having her house vanish like that. She looked around. There was a house with blue curtains in the upstairs bedroom window, and across from it an orange Volkswagen sat in a driveway. There were no blue curtains, no orange Volkswagens on her block. She had turned down the wrong street. No, Hopscotch had. What a stupid place to live, where even a pony could make a mistake.

They were on Mayapple Street. Maryellen Lane was the next one over. Beyond the backyard of the house with the blue curtains she could see the back of the Wilcoxes', their blue swimming pool sticking up beyond the fringe of lombardy poplar trees.

She tried to turn Hopscotch around, to go back to the corner and over and up Maryellen, but the pony stuck her head out and danced sideways. She didn't want to go back. Jean pulled her in a circle and tried again. Hopscotch reared, just a little, her front legs barely off the ground, as a warning. She could do more than that if she had to. She didn't want to go around.

"Pighead," said Jean.

Well, why should they go back when they could go straight through? The house with the blue curtains was quiet, maybe empty, nobody home. Gone to the station to meet her husband. Jean tugged her hat clear to her eyes, crouched down, and kicked the pony. They cantered across

22

the lawn, probably kicking up chunks of grass, along the side of the house, past a swing set and Big Wheel, and through a gap in the poplars to the Wilcoxes' backyard.

Out of nowhere, Mrs. Wilcox sprang up at them, waving a leaf rake.

"Oh, no you don't!" she screamed. "Get out of this yard!"

Hopscotch shied and Jean lost her reins. Thrown off course, too fast to stop, unswerving, they headed for the swimming pool.

Mrs. Wilcox screamed again.

The edge wasn't high, and Hopscotch never hesitated. Neat and clean, with her ears pricked forward, she jumped into the swimming pool and landed with a crashing splash in three feet of water.

Water rose in a great sweeping sheet and soaked Mrs. Wilcox, and Jean fell off into the pool.

4

She scrambled to her feet hanging on to her hat. Water poured down her. Her pockets were bulging with water. It was cold. Icy, bone-aching cold.

Mrs. Wilcox was shrieking with fury. "You get that horse out of there right now! I mean it! Get it out or I'll call the police!" Her pink slacks were sopping. She jabbed angrily at Hopscotch's rump with the rake.

The pony pranced, churning water, and stepped on Jean's foot. She lifted one hind leg as if she might kick her way out.

"I don't think she can jump," chattered Jean. Her teeth were knocking together so hard she could barely speak.

"Suppose she does her business in our swimming pool! You expect Kevin to go swimming in your horse's business?"

Mrs. Reece pushed up her kitchen window to look at the noise, then slammed it shut again and appeared in her doorway carrying the baby. "You'd better get that pony out of there," she shouted, and came trotting across the grass to help. The baby, seeing Hopscotch, started to howl.

"I'll get it out," said Mrs. Wilcox, made braver by reinforcements, and whacked the pony with the rake. Hopscotch pinned her ears back and danced, splashing.

Kevin Wilcox, who was fat and whiny, came out to join them. "I'm going to tell my dad," he told Jean. "He doesn't want you on our property."

Jean climbed out by the ladder with water streaming down her pants legs and her shoes gurgling. She was shivering so hard the ladder trembled. Standing by the side of the pool, she took hold of the reins and pulled, like an idiot. She couldn't think what else to do. "Jump, Hopscotch," she said, without conviction. "Can you jump?"

The pony backed up until she bumped the far side of the pool. The water was over her knees. She had no intention of trying to jump.

"Maybe if we could let the water out," said Jean desperately. "How do you drain it? Is there some kind of stopper or something?"

"We drain it with the hose," said Mrs. Wilcox, dabbing at her slacks with a Kleenex. "It takes eight hours. Make it jump out. If it jumped in, it can jump out."

"If it was a trick pony," said Kevin helpfully, "like the circus, it could go up the ladder."

"She's standing in *water*," cried Jean. "She can't jump."

Mrs. Reece jounced the baby up and down on her arm so its screams came out in bursts, like hiccups. "Maybe if we scare it," she said. *"Aaaaaah!"*

Kevin threw a plastic boat at Hopscotch's head, but it missed. Hopscotch reared, and slipped down, and thrashed back to her feet again.

"Stop that!" cried Jean. She tried to clench her teeth. They were dashing themselves to splinters. Her shoes oozed ice water.

"Boy, you've got some nerve, young lady!" said Mrs. Reece, bobbling her curlers angrily.

For a moment, only for a moment, Jean wished she could simply drop the reins and go home. Leave poor Hopscotch to her fate, and go get out of her clothes. It was too awful, just to stand here freezing to death holding a pony that was trapped in a swimming pool, and everyone screaming at her.

"It sure splashed out a lot of water," said Kevin. "Look at it all. That must've been some splash."

Mrs. Reece and Mrs. Wilcox looked down, and then began to back away. Water was pouring out from under the pool.

Hopscotch's sharp little hoofs had pierced the thin blue plastic liner in a dozen places. The pool was draining fast. A deep puddle spread and grew and seeped away from it across the grass, and some of Kevin's scattered toys began to float.

Mrs. Reece and Mrs. Wilcox kept backing away and staring. The baby continued to scream. Jean stood still, and the water rose around her soaked shoes. Tossing her head and flicking her ears, Hopscotch fidgeted nervously, making the holes bigger. The water found a slant in the lawn and began to run in a stream across the lawn toward the lombardy poplars.

"Maybe I can fix it," said Jean. "Patch it, or something."

"You're crazy," snapped Mrs. Wilcox. "There's about a million holes in there. You'll *replace* it, Jean Monroe, or your mother will, and I mean it. Right away, too."

The water was down to Hopscotch's fetlocks and dropping fast. Jean climbed back down into the pool by the ladder, and sloshed over and dragged herself up onto the pony's back, in soaked pants that stuck to her knees.

26

Could she jump out? It would be safer to take the pool apart, now it was empty and the liner ruined anyway, but Jean didn't want to ask. Mrs. Wilcox would say no anyway. Probably she'd like to see them break their necks.

The bottom was slippery with slime. There was no room for a stride, she'd have to jump it from a standstill, and oh, please, prayed Jean, closing her eyes, don't let her slip and break a leg. Don't let us get killed.

She wrapped her legs around the pony's warm fat ribs. Oh, please, she thought, and gave her a tremendous kick.

Hopscotch crouched down on her back legs like a cat pouncing, and gave a spring that snapped Jean's head back on her neck. *Crack!* The pony hit the edge of the pool, but only with her back legs, not with her knees, her knees to send her sprawling and break her neck on the Wilcoxes' lawn. She landed, and staggered, and gathered herself up again.

Jean kept her eyes shut.

At a brisk, competent trot, like any pony coming home from a day's work, Hopscotch rounded the Monroes' backyard with the Reece baby's screams fading behind her, up the driveway and into her pen.

Jean opened her eyes and sat still for a moment. Safe.

Hopscotch pawed the ground where the hay was kept wrapped in its plastic sheet. It was suppertime.

In the kitchen, Donald was setting the table. "You're late," he said. "I started the potatoes." He focused on her, considering. "You're dripping all over the floor," he observed.

Jean left her clothes in the bathtub, put on dry things, and took four towels out to dry Hopscotch. Her knees still quivered a little, but her teeth had stopped chattering. The pony munched her hay, pausing from time to time for one of those sips of water that emptied half a bucket. Neighbors were no concern of hers. Angry ladies with rakes, ruined swimming pools, mothers, all that human confusion was beneath her notice. She was not a large pony, and she had jumped three feet from a slippery standstill. What more could be expected of her? Now she would eat.

Jean gave her an extra section of hay.

On Tuesdays, the Monroes always had mashed potatoes, meat loaf, and string beans. Jean was supposed to put the meat loaf in the oven and peel and boil the potatoes; Donald mashed them and set the table; their mother, who had made the meat loaf before she went to work, cooked the beans when she got home. Afterwards, Jean cleared the table and scraped the plates and Donald arranged them in the dishwasher.

Wednesdays, macaroni and cheese, spinach, ice cream. Thursdays, fried chicken, with Jean shaking the pieces with flour in a bag and Donald turning them in the pan, thoughtfully, his eyes squinted against the spitting fat.

It was monotonous, but before they had a system it had been worse. Strange meals at all hours, and their mother confused and apologizing, and things from the freezer that hatefully refused to melt, and got charred black on the outside and frozen cold in the middle.

When they got tired of their menus, they all sat down with pencil and paper and worked out some new ones.

Donald mashed the potatoes. Mrs. Monroe came home and changed into her jeans and put the beans on to boil.

I'd better tell her myself, first, thought Jean. Poor Mother. Always something with neighbors. She searched for a way to begin. Her ears felt stretched and achy from listening for the phone.

They sat down. Her mother folded the evening paper into quarters and laid it beside her plate. "Well, my lambs," she said absently. "Did you have a good day?"

Jean cut her meat loaf into little curved sections with her fork. "Not exactly," she began cautiously, and drank some milk.

"Oh Lord," said her mother, turning her paper over. "Another kid's been killed in one of those awful gang fights. Well, whatever else you can't say about Dogwood Estates, at least we don't have teenage gangs."

"Mother," said Jean. "Something happened. . . ."

The phone rang, stabbing Jean's closer ear with a sharp pang. That would be Mr. Wilcox. Too late.

"I'll get it," said Donald.

Mrs. Monroe glanced up. "Don't be long."

Donald took his napkin with him to the living room.

"It says in the paper the price of chicken's going up again. Maybe we'll have to change our Thursdays."

"*Mother,*" said Jean. "Listen, quick. That's Mr. Wilcox. Hopscotch wrecked their stupid swimming pool."

"Really? Good heavens. How?"

"Well, she was in it. She jumped in. And she tore up the plastic lining and we're going to have to get them another one. I'm sorry." Unstrung, her eyes filled with tears.

"Don't cry, lamb. Goodness, how did your *hat* get so wet? Were you in the pool, too?"

She nodded, blinking.

"I hope you changed right away. Are they angry?"

"Yes."

"Oh dear. Maybe we should move to the moon. Jean, you've got to get rid of that pony somehow, we promised, and it's been months and months."

Donald came back.

"Is it Mr. Wilcox?" asked Jean and her mother at the same time.

"Mr. Wilcox?" Donald scowled at his napkin as if trying to remember a Mr. Wilcox. "Why should it be? No, it was

29

Barry." He felt for his chair with his free hand and sat down, still studying his napkin. "R to QB1," he read from it. "R to QB1. Huh."

"Why don't you just go over to Barry's house, Donald, and sit down and play chess with him there?" said his mother. "Wouldn't that be better than using the phone?"

"Better?" Donald looked up, struggling out of the world of chess. "No. We'd have to worry about finishing, and me getting home, and his mother would come fussing around about dinner or something. It makes a more professional game this way. We can take as long as we like."

"How long is this one taking?"

"Hm? I don't remember. September eighth I think we started." He went on with his dinner, his right hand moving neatly and automatically to his mouth while he examined the napkin. "R to QB1," he whispered. "If he thinks I'm going to fall for *that*. . . ."

"Maybe he won't call," said Mrs. Monroe. "Maybe it's all right. Maybe, when she told him about it, he thought it was funny, do you think?"

"Funny?" said Jean. She tried to imagine Mr. Wilcox thinking it was funny, a pony in his pool, but she couldn't. Mr. Wilcox wouldn't think anything was funny, except maybe some television program or something. Of course he was going to call. And yell at her poor mother, who never yelled back at anyone. Maybe he'd even come over, and yell right in their faces, the way nobody would if her father was still alive. If they had a man of some kind around.

If they had somebody who could yell back, or maybe even *hit* him. It was awful just to sit here and let everyone push them around.

She looked at Donald. His face was empty, turned inward to some place where chess pieces moved around in his mind. "I don't see what *use* it is," she said, "having a chess genius for a brother. I wish you were something useful instead. A boxer or a wrestler or something." She tried to think of Donald twisting Mr. Wilcox's arm behind him, forcing him down to the floor, shouting into his face.

"I'm not a chess genius," said Donald, surprised. "It's just for relaxation. I'm a *math* genius. Actually, I'm only a fairly decent chess player. Lots of people are better than I am. There's even a guy right over in Bedlington who's pretty good." He ate some mashed potatoes. They were lumpy. "Some of the guys on the big computers play chess," he added dreamily. "At night, on the computers. Against other computers."

"They've got a computer at our school now," said Jean. "It figures grades and tests and stuff."

"Not *those*," said Donald. "The real computers. Like the one at M.I.T." He stopped, and examined his mother and sister. "Nobody around here ever knows what I'm talking about. I might as well talk to the pony," he said mildly, and addressed himself to his dinner.

"I wish they'd get this Mideast thing settled, one way or another," said Mrs. Monroe to her paper. "I suppose it'll come out all right, but it seems to go on forever."

They finished eating in amiable silence, ponies and neighbors hovering over Jean's mind, computers over Donald's, oil wells and the price of chicken over their mother's. Jean cleared the table.

The phone rang again.

"Oh dear," said Mrs. Monroe. "Oh dear, oh dear, oh *dear*. Well, here goes." She straightened her shoulders and went to answer it.

Jean crouched over the sink, a spray of forks in her hand, rigid. Even Donald stopped fiddling the arrangement of plates in the dishwasher and held still to listen.

Their mother's voice sounded surprised. So it couldn't be

Mr. Wilcox, again. Jean's shoulders relaxed carefully, an inch at a time.

"I see," her mother was saying. "But I talked to you people before. You said you didn't have facilities. You said . . . I see. You mean, if you get a complaint, it makes it different? Yes. Yes, I know, and we were planning to . . . oh. But it's not cold yet, not really cold, and she's well taken care of . . . yes. Yes, but she's *not* . . . oh."

Not Mr. Wilcox. Something else bad. Worse, maybe.

"How long do we have, then? Yes, yes, I know. But what are we supposed to . . . but you aren't giving us any time at all, we have to make arrangements . . . yes, I see. No, I'm sure you won't have to do that. We'll think of something . . . yes, I know. Of course." The phone clicked back into place.

"That," said Mrs. Monroe, coming back, "was the S.P.C.A."

Jean and Donald waited.

Mrs. Monroe sat down at the kitchen table and stared at it. "It seems that Hopscotch is abused and neglected. It seems that a neighbor of ours has called the S.P.C.A. to say his heart was bleeding to see that pony out in the cold." She spread her hands on the table and looked at them as if they were someone else's. "Hopscotch has no place to sleep. No stable. No barn. She's just standing there on the lawn, or what ought to be lawn, and it went down to forty-two degrees last night. Our neighbor is very distressed."

"What are we supposed to *do*?" cried Jean.

"Build a stable," said her mother, and giggled nervously. "*I* don't know. Get rid of her. Right away, quick. Before she gets rained on. Otherwise. . . ."

"What?"

"Otherwise they come get her."

"Get her? But they said, they said already, when you called before, they couldn't keep her."

"I don't suppose they would," said her mother. "Keep her, exactly. I suppose they would . . . put her to sleep." She sighed, and stood up. "I don't know the answer. There isn't any answer." She started toward her bedroom, where she spent the evenings lying on her bed reading murder mysteries, with the radio news station turned down low and murmuring news in her ear.

At the door, she stopped, and added, "You know, I wouldn't have thought Mr. Wilcox was that *smart*. That was a smart thing to do. I'm surprised."

"Check and mate," agreed Donald sadly.

5

You can't go to sleep when your neck is stiff and keeps trying to hold your head up, as if the pillow was a kitten or a wineglass or something that would break if you leaned on it. Jean kept trying to make her neck go limp, and it would, and then it would stiffen up again.

They were going to come and get Hopscotch. They were coming to give her an injection, put her "painlessly to sleep," just the way she'd always pretended to imagine. Now it was real.

"They won't come now," she kept reciting to herself. "They're asleep in bed. They won't come at night. She's safe. She's perfectly safe till morning. They won't come now."

But she couldn't sleep. She couldn't bring her attention in from the front yard. Most of herself was out there, floating anxiously over the dark pony pen, and wouldn't come back in and roll up soft and go to sleep. She strained to hear sounds. The gerbils rustled in their cage. A car going by stiffened her all over.

She heard something. She really did. A rattling noise.

34

Some kind of chain, maybe? For dragging dead ponies?

She rolled out of bed and wrapped the blanket around her and crept downstairs barefoot. Another noise, a sort of muffled crash.

The kitchen light was on. She gathered up the tails of the blanket and padded in on cold feet. It was her mother.

"Good heavens, you scared me," said Mrs. Monroe.

"You scared me. I heard something. I thought they were coming for Hopscotch."

"In the middle of the night?"

"Yes. What are you doing?"

"I thought I'd make some doughnuts."

"In the middle of the night?"

Mrs. Monroe laughed, and wiped her hands on the seat of her blue jeans, leaving floury streaks. "I couldn't sleep. 'Preheat fat to 370 degrees.'"

"Mother, what are we going to *do*? About Hopscotch?"

"I wish I knew. I wish I could think of something."

Jean sat on the table with her feet on a chair, and pulled the blanket tight around her shoulders and stared at the little red light on the deep-fat fryer that meant it was heating. The smell of hot oil, slightly fishy, floated through the kitchen. Doughnuts. As if that would help. You couldn't build a stable out of doughnuts.

She clenched her jaw on a fierce wave of anger at her mother. Mothers were supposed to have answers. Even if it was a terrible answer, not what you wanted to do at all, they had to think of *something*. That's what they were for.

"Everyone picks on us," she said. "It's because we don't have a husband here. They think we're weird, and helpless."

"'Dip spatula in hot fat.' Okay, it's dipped. Don't feel that way, Jeannie. They're not exactly picking on us. It's just that this isn't really a good place for ponies."

"They want everyone to be like them. They don't want anyone to have something they don't have, or do anything they don't. Like you working. If you do anything different they jump all over you." She tugged angrily at her hat. "I wish you'd get married. To somebody with a *gun*."

The light on the fryer went out. Her mother, biting her lip, slid a flat, raw doughnut down into the spitting fat. "I've never made doughnuts before. Look, it *is* puffing up."

"They're going to taste like fish. Mother, why don't you get married?"

"Nobody's asked me. 'Never crowd the frying kettle.' It does smell kind of fishy, doesn't it?"

"Fish doughnuts. Yum."

"If you've never tried them, don't knock them. Jeannie, I don't know anyone to marry, and even if I did, I'm not sure I'd want to. The only men I see are the neighbors, and Mr. Allenbee at the museum. Mr. Allenbee's past seventy, they keep asking him politely to retire, but he just turns off his hearing aid and keeps on puttering around the cabinets. Hand me the paper towels. I'm not a glamorous young mother like in the commercials, lamb. I'm forty-two years old. Look." She bent over to show Jean the gray hairs in the crown of her head. "I think this first one's done."

She lifted it out, puffed and brown, and laid it on the paper towels. "It *looks* pretty, anyway. Photograph it and throw it away, as your father used to say."

"If you got married, maybe we could even live somewhere else."

"Another thing, we're all kind of set in our ways. All three of us. It'd have to be a pretty unusual man to put up with us the way we are. We'd probably have to change."

"How?"

Mrs. Monroe lifted out three more doughnuts and put

them on the paper towels, and sniffed them suspiciously. Then she said, "Oh, I don't know, lamb. Donald join the football team. You stop wearing that hat. Me quit work. He'd probably be allergic to ponies. Anyway, there isn't any 'he.' "

"You could kind of . . . fix yourself up? Get some clothes, or something. Lipstick." Jean waved vaguely, and the blanket slid off her shoulders.

"Oh, Jean, stop nagging. I've *been* married, and very happily, too. Now I'm very happy dusting my butterflies and poking around in my blue jeans. Without lipstick. Maybe when you kids leave I'll be so lonesome I'll marry Mr. Allenbee. He'll be about a hundred by then. I can push him around in his wheelchair. But in the meantime—ow!" She had splashed some hot fat, and sucked her wrist. "In the meantime," she mumbled, "no."

Jean sighed. "Then maybe we could just move. I mean, we don't *have* to live here, do we?"

"Well, kind of. If it wasn't here, it would be someplace just like here. The kind of houses we can afford are houses in places like this. It's cheaper to build a whole lot just alike. Here, want one?"

Jean took a doughnut and smelled it, and bit into it. Her mother watched her. "Fishy?" she asked.

"Not much. Sort of soggy, though."

"Oh."

They each ate two.

"Shall I throw the rest away?"

"Donald'll eat them," said Jean. "For breakfast. He doesn't care what he eats."

"Cold fish doughnuts." Mrs. Monroe wrapped them in a paper towel and put them by Donald's place at the table. "I'm going to bed." She stretched and yawned widely, showing her fillings. "And Jeannie. Try not to feel too bad about Hopscotch. Maybe everything'll be all right. And if it isn't . . . well, you did have her all summer."

Jean turned her face bitterly away from her mother and felt her eyes fill up with tears. Mrs. Monroe waited a minute, as if she was hoping to find something better to say, and then shrugged sadly and left the room.

Jean sat on the table and stared at the sink. The tap dripped, very slowly, one drip, count to eight, then another drip, count to eight. The doughnuts hunched in her stomach like a stone. In the curtainless kitchen window she could see her face, looking pointy and fierce under her hat, like one of those little animals that live in holes and have sharp teeth.

Outside, beyond the window, nothing was safe. Anyone who could untie knots in clothesline could take Hopscotch away and kill her. Because Mr. Wilcox was smarter than they'd thought. Because nobody on Maryellen Lane wanted Jean Monroe to have a pony, or anything else that was different or strange.

Inside, at least she was safe. She could lock the doors.

A pony would be safe inside too.

Jean slid abruptly down from the table, losing her blanket.

It was too bad she couldn't use the garage. The garage would be perfect, except that their old car was delicate and had to stay dry or else it wouldn't start. However, there was the laundry room.

She flicked on the light and looked around. Plenty of room, really. She lifted the dribbling basket of dirty clothes up onto the dryer, pushed the vacuum cleaner into a corner, and set the trash basket on the washing machine. Plenty of room. There was a pile of old Sunday papers under the laundry tub, and she spread some out on the floor, for bedding, and got a carrot from the refrigerator and went out.

Hopscotch whickered in the dark. Jean held the flashlight pinned under her arm and struggled with the clothesline knots. Curious, the pony crowded over to watch, and her sweet breath whispered warmly on Jean's neck.

It was cold. Across the street, the Pikes had a light on in the living room, shining through the white curtains of their picture window, and another light in the upstairs bathroom. They weren't awake, though. The Pikes were afraid of burglars, and always kept lights on. All the other houses on Maryellen Lane were dark. Nobody was watching *The Late Show*, no child was sick, nobody else's mother was making doughnuts.

Jean, shivering in her pajamas and hat, led Hopscotch softly across the grass, then clopping over the concrete strip of driveway, and around back to the door. The laundry room was a glare of lightness, and the pony stopped short and blinked in at it.

"It's okay," said Jean. "Come on. We haven't got all night." She pulled on the clothesline lead rope.

Hopscotch put her head politely into the house and looked around, ears sharp with curiosity. "Come *on*!" Delicately, lifting her small feet over the threshold, she stepped in and followed Jean over to the laundry tub and peered down into it.

"You're going to have to be tied up," said Jean. "I'm sorry. But just stand still and go to sleep, okay?" She filled the laundry tub with water, and tied the clothesline in several hard knots to the faucet.

Hopscotch backed nervously into the shelves of canned stuff and knocked some soup onto the floor. Jean retrieved the cans. "Stand *still*, and you'll be all right. You're safe in here, for tonight, anyway. Tomorrow we'll think of something else."

The pony drank some water from the laundry tub and pressed her dripping muzzle on Jean's shoulder. Jean arranged the blond forelock neatly between her eyes, and played with the little fur-lined ears. "We'll figure something out in the morning," she promised. "We won't let them get you. Even if we have to run away."

She locked the outside door and turned off the light, and paused a moment to listen to Hopscotch's feet, fidgeting restlessly in the newspapers. Then she went to bed, and dreamed all night of terrible alarms and dangers, things chasing her, fires; the pursued and helpless nightmares of a four-year-old.

In the morning, she woke up with a feeling of emergency. People were shouting. Something crashed. She was in a ship, and it was sinking, they were getting into lifeboats. No, it was a train. It was falling off a high trestle across a mountain pass, falling slowly, peeling away off the trestle, car by car, and dropping endlessly down to the rocks below. Her mother was there. She could hear her voice.

Then she woke up completely, and leaped out of bed and ran downstairs.

Donald was saying, "I think you scared her, yelling like that."

The laundry room was a wreck. Hopscotch had knocked over a lot of cans, and pulled the laundry basket off the dryer, and she was rearing and backing and pulling on her rope, slipping on cans and tangling her feet in the rumple of sheets and torn paper. The faucet rocked and groaned as she pulled on it.

"Stop that!" cried Mrs. Monroe. "Donald, get her *out*.

40

Untie that thing. Watch out, she'll kick!" Hopscotch's ears were back flat.

Jean squeezed quickly past them, and dived for the rope.

"*You're* here," said her mother. "Get that animal out of here, Jean Monroe. She's tearing out the plumbing. Hurry up!"

Jean, with her hands on the clothesline, stopped to stare at her mother. Her mother never talked like that. That was the kind of thing other people's mothers said, Mrs. Reece and people like that. Her mother never yelled, never told people to do something they were perfectly obviously doing already. Jean was hurt, and furious. She turned back and untied the rope, coaxing and pulling the pony forward to ease up on it.

"Get her *out*."

There was no room to turn her around. Jean pressed against her chest and mumbled, "Back. Back, Hop. Back."

Nervous, Hopscotch lifted her lovely, fawn-colored tail and pooped on the floor.

"Oh, God *damn* it," said Mrs. Monroe. And she went back into the kitchen.

Donald was helpfully trying to pick up cans and laundry.

"How's she supposed to get out with you in the way?" said Jean nastily.

"Clean it up yourself, then." Donald threw a T-shirt on the floor and stalked out. Jean would have liked to cry with despair if she hadn't been so angry. Everyone was horrible.

"Jean," said her mother from the kitchen, "you aren't going out there in your pajamas?"

"I thought you wanted Hopscotch out. How else am I supposed to take her?"

She maneuvered the pony out backward, bumping the door, and walked barefoot in the cold morning air around the house with her. The ground was so cold it burned like fire. Mrs. Pike, in her doorway in a wrapper bringing in the milk, stopped to stare suspiciously at her. Two cars went by, slowly, the drivers staring.

Defiantly, Jean took her time feeding Hopscotch, and filled her water bucket, and tied the clothesline fence up carefully, her hands shaking. Mrs. Wilcox came to her bedroom window and shouted something, but Jean refused to look around.

Back in the house, Donald was collecting his schoolbooks with a cold doughnut in his teeth, and her mother was drinking coffee.

"I'm sorry I yelled at you, lamb."

Jean poured herself a glass of orange juice and drank it standing up at the sink, her back to her mother. From the kitchen window she could see into the Wilcoxes' kitchen window. Kevin was burrowing in a cereal box for something, one of those things that come in cereal and never work. Over in their backyard, the ruined swimming pool stared at her like a horrible blue eye.

"Jeannie? I'm sorry. I've got a headache, and I didn't sleep well. I was just feeling . . . badgered. Neighbors and things."

Jean looked over her shoulder coldly. "How do you suppose *I* feel?"

"I know. It's worse for you."

Jean didn't answer. She put her glass in the dishwasher and went upstairs to dress, forcing her feet into damp, stiff shoes.

The front door banged as Donald went out to catch the early school bus. Then the garage door groaned and rattled, the car coughed and started, and her mother drove away to catch the 8:22.

42

Jean was the last to leave in the mornings, locking doors, checking lights and the thermostat. It was Wednesday, macaroni and cheese, nothing to take from the freezer.

She looked grimly into the laundry room, and went to get paper towels for the poop before starting on the newspapers and cans and dirty socks, and the spilled laundry soap.

Through the picture window she could see Hopscotch eating her breakfast, selecting a bite of hay and jerking her head up to free it from the pile, then munching steadily and peacefully as she watched the morning cars go by beside her pen.

Brian Harrison and some other boy passed on their way to the school bus, and the other boy stopped a moment to shoot a paper clip at Hopscotch with a rubber band. It hit her on the shoulder, and she shook her head in surprise. She had probably been hit with several hundred paper clips, there were always some in her pen, but it never stopped surprising her. She never seemed to connect the quick sting with the passing child; why should anyone want to hurt her? She continued to watch the boys as they moved away, her ears pricked with cheerful interest, munching.

When they came from the S.P.C.A., Jean thought, with an injection to kill her, chop her right down in the beginning of her life, she'd run right over to them. They wouldn't have to chase her around the pen with ropes, or hold her. She wouldn't try to escape. She'd trot up to them whickering, pleased with herself as always, pleased to have company, and push at their pockets for carrots.

She'd be easy to kill.

Jean put the cans back on the shelves, and the dirty clothes in the washing machine, and wiped up the poop. The laundry-tub faucet was definitely bent, but it still worked. She was picking up the last of the torn newspaper when she heard the school bus wheezing to a stop at Wisteria Drive, and the bat-squeak of its brakes.

She straightened up and looked at the wall in momentary panic, her mouth open. She'd missed the bus.

But then, she wasn't going to school anyway. She couldn't, not just go off, and come back and find the pen empty and the gate ties dangling, and never know anything more.

She had to stay with Hopscotch and . . . what? Hide her in the laundry room again and say she's been sold? But a pony can't stay locked up forever in a laundry room, and the Wilcoxes would call again, and the S.P.C.A. would come back.

On the other hand, she couldn't just sit here and watch from the window, and wait and be helpless. Watch while the pony, trapped in her pen, trotted up to them all friendly and cheerful, and then died.

She had to be hidden. Maybe there was a place somewhere, on beyond the new houses, where she could tie her up in the woods, just for a little while, until she could find something better.

She got her bridle from the kitchen drawer and a carrot from the refrigerator and went out.

6

Hopscotch clip-clopped softly across the sidewalk and down toward Wisteria Drive, toward the hill and the new houses. She mouthed her bit and turned her head from side to side, interested in the different shapes and shadows of things now, in the morning, instead of their usual afternoon look. Mrs. Simmers, leaving in her car for morning errands, slowed down to glare. Jean pulled at her hat and clenched her jaw.

Everyone else was in school. There was no one in all the streets of Dogwood Estates except mothers and babies in strollers, bundled up securely in the mild fall sunshine.

If she tied Hopscotch up in the woods somewhere, how would she feed her? How could she carry the hay up, or water? And suppose someone found her there, and thought she was abandoned?

Jean looked back over her shoulder at her own house. If only I could build a stable, she thought. But she hadn't any money left, and boards cost a fortune. Besides, she'd had a lot of experience building things, and they always fell down, crushing whoever was in them. Mr. Wilcox wouldn't be too crazy about a homemade stable, either, even if it didn't fall down.

Something else, then. *Something.*

If you won a pony, you got to keep it. If you won a pony in a magazine contest, after everyone, Shelley and even your own mother, said nobody ever won those contests; if you actually did keep on trying till you won it, then it was silly to think you'd have to get rid of it. It was insane, it was just *not true* that people could come and kill it. Things didn't end that way. It would be like the enchanted prince slaying the dragon and marrying the princess, and then they couldn't stand each other and got a divorce.

They turned up the hill, going nowhere except away. Jean bent over the muscling shoulders, along the road where bulldozers had gouged herringbone ruts in the mud, past the first new houses on the smooth, oily stretch of finished road. Farther up, machinery was grinding, something big backing and straining.

Suddenly, beside them, from one of the new houses, came the battering machine-gun rattle of a compression hammer.

Hopscotch sprang sideways, wrenching Jean over her shoulder, and wheeled and ran.

She jumped the sewer pipe at the side of the road, with Jean clutching her neck, more off than on, and bounded up the bank in wild lurches, like a rabbit.

Jean grabbed with her legs and held on fiercely, and crouched low to hide her face as they tore crashing into the woods.

Branches smacked and lashed her. She bent over double, grabbing at neck and mane to stay on. The reins swung loose and snatched at twigs and bushes. A bird flew up screeching under their feet.

46

It was scrubby woods, all prickers and whippy branches. Jean's knees were banged and scraped. Hopscotch tripped and stumbled and almost fell, and kept crashing and stumbling on. Jean was clutching her neck as if to choke her, while the rest of her lurched and banged from side to side.

Something cracked her on the head and tore at her hat, but she grabbed it back with one hand.

Without warning, Hopscotch crouched and sprang over a fallen tree, and Jean fell off backward.

She landed in soft, leafy dirt that knocked the breath out of her, and lay gasping. The pony stopped, and circled back to nose at her. Jean caught the dangling reins.

Branches and leaves were snagged in the flaxen mane. White sweat foamed on her shoulders.

"It's okay," said Jean, when she could speak. "Ssh. It's okay. It's not chasing us."

Hopscotch's sides were heaving. Jean picked herself up and groaned. "I hurt all over," she said. "I bet you do too."

The pony pressed her face against Jean's chest and blew a warm gasping sigh through her sweater and shirt. She was a brave and sensible pony, and she was not afraid of delivery trucks or dogs or baby carriages, bicycle horns, lawn mowers, or boys with cap pistols or paper clips. Compression hammers, however, were something else again. Jean rubbed the pony's ears.

"I don't know where we are," she said. They were standing on a faint track through the scrubby woods, a double path, such as might have been made by farm wagons in some faraway time. Sassafras and wineberries had grown up in the middle of it. Hopscotch pulled up a mouthful of weeds, shook the dirt from their roots, and munched them, dribbling green foam.

"Well, there isn't any sense going back," said Jean. "We couldn't find our way back through that mess, anyway. We might as well see where this goes."

Her knee hurt, and it seemed too much trouble to get back on Hopscotch again. She walked along the track with the pony following her, reins swinging loose between them except when Hopscotch paused to taste the dusty, faded weeds and jerked Jean's arm.

The track went up to the top of the hill. There, through a dead tree, like a crooked finger pointing at the blue sky, was a stone chimney in what had once been a clearing in the woods. It curved out to a fireplace at the bottom, stained with smoke. In front of it the cellar hole was a jumble of fallen logs and stones, tangled in honeysuckle. Nothing else around seemed human except a straggling patch of day lilies, a broken bottle, and a blue enamelware coffeepot with a hole in the bottom.

Like a stubborn dog, Hopscotch pulled back on the reins till the bridle threatened to slip over her ears.

"What's the matter?" asked Jean. She dropped the coffeepot. There were spiders in it. "Ghosts? Snakes?"

It did look snaky. There was no sense ruling out ghosts, either.

Something rolled under Jean's foot, and she bent down and picked it up, and rubbed the dirt off on her pants. It was a doll's head, a china doll's head, completely bald, and white except for its round insane-looking blue eyes.

Whoever lived here had had a little girl.

Jean looked into the blue eyes. Real people, *real* people, had lived here.

It made her feel quite peculiar, to think of them living so differently. You got used to Dogwood Estates, she thought, and you got to feeling everyone lived there and lived like that and always had. At school, in geography or history, you learned what the book said about different people, but you knew perfectly well it wasn't really true. They weren't *really* people, just pictures, in silly clothes.

Beyond the abandoned chimney a narrow footpath went twisting away down the hill. Feet had worn it down so tree roots came bulging through.

People had lived here for a long time. They had worn a wagon trail up to their house. They had gone down that path for something, over and over, wearing it down. They made coffee in a blue pot, and played with a doll.

Hopscotch pulled back on the reins harder, and pawed angrily in the leaves and lilies.

"Oh, all *right*," said Jean. "Sissy." She put the doll's head in her pocket.

They went down the twisted footpath, through thicker woods with bigger trees. Hopscotch stumbled on the roots.

"Pick up your feet," said Jean. "You're a sidewalk pony, that's your trouble."

They came to the spring that was the reason for the path. It was set around with stones, and a rusty saucepan with no handle was lying beside it. Hopscotch nosed the dead leaves aside and drank. The people had come down here for water, and carried it in buckets back up to the house.

After the spring there was no more path, and Jean pushed through the woods, holding the branches back to keep from snapping Hopscotch in the face.

Ahead of them she could see light. "We're coming to something. Maybe it's a road."

At the edge of the woods, through a scatter of red dogwoods and prickers, they came out into an overgrown field. The grass was higher than Hopscotch's knees, and raggedy with goldenrod and red sumac.

Across the round curve of the field she could see a piece of highway, and hear a truck purring down it. In her mind, the world lurched around and righted itself. She knew where she was, sort of. That highway was Route 9. Out of sight to the left it went past Valleyvista Acres, where Kim Alexander lived, and Jerry Steiff, and Heather Williams; the school bus stopped there. In the other direction, beyond the woods to the right, was the way to the bank and the shopping center and the place to get the car fixed.

Hopscotch lifted her head and whinnied—a long, trumpeting, shuddering whinny that shook her all over.

Jean looked where she was looking. Below them, settled into the hillside, was a big white house and a red barn. A long driveway lined with maples went down the hill, across a creek, past a little stone house and out to a narrow road. Beside the drive was a field full of ponies. She counted. Five ponies, no, six. Hopscotch pulled on the reins and pranced in a circle.

"Wait for me," said Jean. She hoisted herself up, scrambling into place just as the pony broke into a trot, and then a canter, splashing through weeds and brambles.

They stopped at the fence, or what had once been a rail fence but was buckling now under a tumbled mass of honeysuckle vines. Two white-gray ponies trotted up. Their forelocks were tangled and lumpy with burrs, but they seemed friendly. Hopscotch nickered, and yearned across the honeysuckle toward them.

"Poor baby," said Jean, pulling twigs out of the flaxen mane. "You've been lonesome, haven't you? I bet you thought you were the last pony left in the world."

A tiny bay, its tail a single clump of burrs, came slowly and warily toward them, limping, poised to run away, and the other three followed it, curious, excited, pleased, and nervous. The bay touched noses with Hopscotch, and kicked and wheeled away, and then came edging back.

Clouds passed over the sun, and the shadows of them

50

moved slowly as water across the curving field. The maple trees along the driveway were red and gold, like peaches, and down by the road the little stone house was half hidden in red and gold leaves.

"Hopscotch Monroe," said Jean, "wouldn't it be lovely if you could come and live here?"

Why not? Surely, surely, anyone with a field and a barn and six ponies already wouldn't mind seven? Even if it cost money, it couldn't be much. Not like a proper stable. She could work and earn it somehow. Babysitting, maybe, although Shelley got all the sitting jobs on Maryellen Lane. Raking leaves, maybe.

"Let's go ask," she said. But Hopscotch was happy where she was, talking in little nips and whickers and ear-flickings with the others. Jean had to get down and pull up a tough stalk of goldenrod for a switch before she could get her away from the fence.

They followed the fence line, and the ponies straggled along behind them on the other side. Around the barn, past an ancient truck with vines growing over its doors, they came down to the back of the big white house, and suddenly they were drowned in a wave of barking dogs milling wildly around them.

Hopscotch flattened her ears and reared.

Jean pulled her in a circle, shouting "Shut up! Shut up!" at the dogs. I'm going to fall off in a minute, she thought, and they'll eat me. There seemed to be hundreds of them. The noise was maddening. She hit Hopscotch as hard as she could with the goldenrod, and the pony sprang out through them. They clattered over the driveway and up to the house, pursued by furious dogs.

They'll know I'm here, anyway, thought Jean. What a stupid way to come visiting. Like Paul Revere.

At the doorstep, she half-slid, half-fell off the pony, down into the dogs. They yammered and howled as if they might tear her apart, but their tails were wagging. "Quiet!" she screamed. "Shut *up*!" Hopscotch swung her head among them, baring her teeth.

There was no doorbell, but a heavy brass knocker, and Jean banged it as hard as she could, though if they hadn't heard the dogs by now they must be dead, she thought.

Hopscotch kicked a dog, and it yelped and ran, and circled and came back, still barking. No one answered the door. Jean banged again.

Suddenly the door opened inward, under her hand, and she let go of the knocker, feeling like a fool. A dumpy little gray-haired lady stood in the doorway, gazing out at the tangle of dogs and girl and pony with mild interest. She said nothing.

"Excuse me," said Jean. "I . . . I wondered . . ." and words failed her. She felt completely off balance, stupid with confusion. The dogs roared, and she stared at the woman with her mouth open.

The woman clapped her hands. The dogs fell into instant silence, and furled their tails and slunk off under the boxwood bushes like the ghosts of dogs.

It was so quiet you could hear cars on Route 9. Hopscotch jerked some leaves off a rhododendron and ate them.

"Excuse me," Jean tried again. "I thought, I mean, is there somebody here I could ask about keeping a pony? Here, I mean?"

"I'm afraid there isn't anyone here but me."

Jean blushed hotly. Was she someone to ask? Was it her house, or was she the maid, maybe, or what? She looked like no one Jean had ever met before. Her short gray hair looked as if she cut it herself, in the dark probably, and her blue dress hung shapelessly down over her legs. Even her shoes looked homemade. Her face had the soft, formless look of a child's face, and her mild eyes looked out through rimless glasses as if she were trying to remember somebody's name, or the date of the Boston Tea Party.

I could just go away, thought Jean. But she couldn't, of course. This was the place for Hopscotch. If there was any answer, if she had been headed for anywhere at all today, this had to be the answer and the place.

She took a deep breath, and said, "Please, I'd like to board my pony here."

"Won't you come in, then?" said the woman. "You can tie the little mare up, the dogs won't bother her."

At least she said "mare," thought Jean, and "her." Most people said "him" or "it." That was a good sign.

There was a hitching post by the door, a plain real one, not one of those stupid little black-boys-in-red-coats holding out their hands, such as the Simmers had for nothing at all but dogs to pee on. She tied the reins to the ring. Hopscotch looked over her shoulder at the pony field.

Jean pulled her hat down solidly around her ears and followed the woman into the house.

7

They went past dark, shadowy rooms that seemed to be full of big, dark furniture. Jean tiptoed. Maybe she's a witch, she thought childishly. That's where the ponies came from. Six other girls have come here, at different times, looking for a place for their ponies, and one by one she killed and ate them and kept the ponies.

At the end of the house was the kitchen, and the woman stopped. Jean looked around, furtively, under her hat. There was an enormous fireplace full of trash, with a rusty iron hook dangling in it, a big, dark table that didn't look as if it belonged in a kitchen, and two rickety wooden chairs. A jelly jar on the windowsill held a bunch of black-eyed susans shedding their yellow petals down into the sink.

"You must excuse me," said the woman. "I don't get many visitors."

"I don't mean to . . . intrude," said Jean. "It's just—"

"I'm Alicia Remington," she went on, as if Jean hadn't spoken. "Alicia *S.* Remington, that is. I was a Shaw before I married."

Jean smiled blankly. Did she say Shah, she wondered,

54

like the Shah of Iran? She tried to imagine the woman in a burnoose, on a camel. "I'm Jean Monroe."

"Delighted to meet you. Would you care for a little sherry?"

"No, thank you," said Jean, alarmed. And then, "I mean, I don't know. I never tried it. Yes, please." She took the glass, which was smudged and a little sticky in her hand.

"Your health," said Alicia Remington. "Cheers, as they say in England."

A smoke-gray Persian cat sprang softly up onto the table and picked its way over to rub against Jean, purring. Its fur was matted and hung on its sides in chunks.

"Cheers," said Jean awkwardly. The sherry had a stern, serious, grown-up taste, like the prescription cough medicine you got when you were very sick indeed. She swallowed with difficulty, and coughed. The cat sniffed at her glass.

"*Her* name," said Mrs. Remington, "is Cleo."

"Hello, Cleo," said Jean.

She moved an open box of crackers and a Sears catalog to make a space to put her glass down. There was a silence. The kitchen smelled of bread mold and the sooty, chimney smell of last winter's fires. She had to get the conversation back where it belonged. "The thing is," she said desperately, "I have this pony. I won it, in a contest."

"You won a contest? You must be a very fortunate person. I've never known anyone who won contests. Perhaps you were born under propitious influences. When's your birthday?"

"April third. But—"

"Ah, an Aries. That explains it."

"But the thing is, I don't have any place to keep her. The pony. I live in Dogwood Estates."

Mrs. Remington made a face like a baby that hates its cereal. "Frightful place. This shopping center business is all because of them, you know. They're expanding it."

"I know. But the neighbors mind my keeping Hopscotch in the yard. She got into Mr. Wilcox's swimming pool, and he called the S.P.C.A. So, I mean, I came here by accident, and I noticed you had some ponies."

"My freeloaders." Mrs. Remington smiled tenderly and finished her sherry.

"And I wondered how much you charge for boarding. I could come and ride her, it isn't very far. At least I don't think it is."

"More sherry? Are you sure? Oh, I don't charge them anything. Actually, I suppose you might say they're mine. I found the two grays at an auction, where even the man from the cat-food place didn't want them. I paid five dollars for each. You should have seen that smaller one. Ribs like barrel hoops, and mange, too, poor thing. Abused, you know." She sighed, and poured herself more sherry. "Don't lick the frying pan, Cleo. What was I saying? Oh, ponies. The little brown one's been foundered, and he's no use at all. The man was going to have him shot. And the chestnut. . . ." She frowned into her glass. "To tell you the truth, I forget where the chestnut came from. If you have a place for them, you know, ponies just tend to appear. Reminds me of my husband, of course. Having them around."

"But what about *Hopscotch*?" cried Jean. "Could I keep Hopscotch here, too?"

"Your pony? Heavens, child—I'm sorry, I forget your name."

"Jean Monroe."

"The trouble is, Jean, I won't be here very much longer. I don't really know what's to become of the ones I've got already."

56

Jean, embarrassed, bent her head and stroked the cat. Did she mean she was going to die? That she was sick with something? She looked okay. Weird, but not sick.

"It's this shopping center thing, as I said before. They want the land." Mrs. Remington gazed out through the cobwebby window and her square baby's face looked wistful. "My poor land," she murmured. "Never any good, really, not for farming. Just a little corn, but then we never expected any more, never had to. There was always money. Never put your money in railroad stocks, Joan. Of course, you couldn't have told my poor husband that. His family *always* had railroad stocks. The Shaws," she added proudly, "were always in utilities. But of course that's all gone now, too."

"I don't understand," said Jean. "The shopping center people want to buy it?"

"Certainly. It's because of your Dogwood what-do-you-call-it? Expanding, you know. More houses. You'd think there were plenty of shopping centers already."

"But you don't have to sell it to them. Do you?"

Mrs. Remington looked suspiciously into the bottom of her sherry glass as if there were little things in it. "It's the taxes," she explained. "Thank heavens my poor husband never lived to see the taxes doubled like that, and then doubled again, what with housing developments needing all those schools, and highways, and sewers, and heaven knows what. So you see, Joan, Jean, if you leave your poor little mare here, she's likely to be cemented over to make a parking lot. Cheers."

"But it won't happen right away?"

"Well, not today. I don't know when, really. My lawyer's very meticulous, keeps going over things with a magnifying glass, and there's all this hemming and hawing. But it has to come soon. Taxes are taxes." Mrs. Remington ran water into her glass and put the sherry bottle back into the cupboard, closing the door firmly as if it might escape. "If you can't pay them, you know, you have to sell. Nothing else to do."

"Then, is it all right to leave Hopscotch here, just until it . . . happens?"

Mrs. Remington looked momentarily confused, as if she had forgotten what they were talking about. "Oh, your pony?" she said. "Why, I don't know, really."

"But I have to leave her *somewhere*!"

"Why, then, I don't see why not, I suppose. As long as you understand it's temporary. But then everything's temporary, isn't it? Come along, I'll show you the gate."

She went into the passage by the kitchen and took a man's raincoat, very dirty around the cuffs and pockets, from a hook on the wall. "Perhaps you'll bring me some luck, you and your lucky pony. Highmeadow's used up its own. Luck, you know."

Outside, the hitching post was empty. They found Hopscotch, broken reins dangling, over by the fence with her head propped across the tangle of vines, visiting.

Jean knotted the reins together. That made two knots. She'd hardly be able to reach them.

Mrs. Remington trudged along the fence, shorter than Jean in her strange square-looking shoes. The dogs followed them. Hopscotch whinnied, and her new friends straggled after them on the other side of the fence.

The gate had sagged with years and weather, and you had to brace your shoulder under the top bar and lift while you pushed. "Hold on," said Jean. "Wait. Let me get your bridle off."

Freed, Hopscotch galloped halfway up the hillside, and then buckled her legs and lay down and rolled, back and forth, flourishing her hoofs in the air and scratching her back on the short, stony grass. Excited, the others trotted in circles and nipped each other.

"She likes it here," said Jean.

"They like company."

Jean glanced at her shyly. "Do you ride much?" It was hard to imagine.

"Oh, heavens, no. Never. My husband did, of course. Hunted. Always kept hunters. Well. . . ." And she turned and started back to the house. The visit was over.

Jean stood in the maple-lined driveway with her bridle in her hand. She felt a long way from home. Hundreds of miles, probably. All her bruises ached. "Excuse me," she said. Mrs. Remington looked around. "I'm not sure about getting home. That *is* Route 9 down there, isn't it?"

"That's Route 9. Ghastly. I can hear the trucks at night."

"And . . . and I go that direction?"

"Where did you say you lived, child?"

"Dogwood Estates."

"Heavens, don't take Route 9. That's the long way. You want to go up the road here to Township Line, and across that way."

"Township Line?" Jean's shoulders sagged with despair. She had never heard of it.

"Why, perhaps I should drive you." Mrs. Remington looked as if this were an odd and unusual idea. "Yes, I could do that. Just a minute, I'll get the car." And she trudged stiffly off up the driveway, followed by dogs.

Jean, since she hadn't been asked to come, sat down in the dusty grass under the maples to wait.

Up on the hillside, the big white house sat wide and solid, gazing out over its fields. Beside it the barn, into which Mrs. Remington and the dogs were disappearing, sagged alarmingly to one side. The stone bottom of it looked firm, but the board part had a chewed-on look under its brave red paint. Swallows flew in and out of a hole in the roof.

The driveway ran down the hill and across the stream on a rackety plank bridge, golden maples on either side, past Jean to the road and the little stone house.

Whose was the little house? It looked as if it should have people in it, children to climb the big cherry tree behind it and chickens to scratch in its yard, but the small panes of its windows held nothing but the reflection of trees. Weeds grew up to the front door. It seemed to be wading in weeds.

Someone should live there, thought Jean. *I* should live there. She hugged her knees, trying to imagine it. It was silly, like pretending to live in a cave, or a tepee. Nobody lived in places like that any more, with a cherry tree and a tilting outhouse in back, half-buried under lilac bushes. People had, though. Once. She felt the lump of the bald doll's head in her pocket.

With considerable roaring and backfiring, a jeep zig-zagged backwards out of the barn and came leaping down the driveway toward her, canvas sides fluttering.

"Climb in," said Mrs. Remington.

"Thank you very much," said Jean, remembering her manners. The canvas door on her side wouldn't shut, so she held it closed, and propped her feet up on an empty oil can.

"Not very comfortable, I'm afraid."

"I think it's neat," said Jean. "I've never been in a jeep before." The jeep sprang forward, snapping her neck.

"It was my husband's. He brought it back. He was a colonel, you know, in the war."

What war? Mrs. Remington seemed to think there was only one, so she didn't ask.

The mailbox at the road said HIGHMEADOW. A. S. REMINGTON.

"Doesn't anyone live in the little stone house?"

"Oh, gracious no. It's not what they call modernized. No plumbing. It's the tenant house, for the caretaker, you know, the hired man. Or it was; we haven't had anyone since . . . oh, heavens, I can't remember. The last one was that Jerry, that got in all the trouble with the police. When was that—1956, maybe? Or '55? Everything's been falling apart ever since. The barn'll be the next thing to go, I'm afraid." She sounded sorrowful, but not as if anything much could be done about it. Hired men left and barns fell down, and shopping centers came, and she watched it all as if it was weather. Something nobody could help.

"Couldn't the barn be fixed?" asked Jean. "Kind of braced up, or something?"

"Oh, I doubt it." She swerved wildly around a hole in the road, and Jean grabbed at the roof to keep from falling out. "No use, anyway. Fix it up for the bulldozers."

The jeep was like riding a half-trained horse, Jean thought. It might bolt any minute, or toss you into the ditch. It had hard gaits, too. She clenched her teeth to keep from biting her tongue.

From Township Line Road they came into Dogwood Estates at a different angle, down at the far end of Azalea. It was strange, seeing it from here, like looking at a familiar view from upside down. All those acres of houses, white and green and white and tan. Her eyes felt unused to them. After just that little time at Highmeadow, suddenly Dogwood Estates seemed a distinctly weird place to live. It looked sad, she thought, and kind of scary, and lonely. All squeezed in together staring into each other's windows like mirrors, and everyone lonesome and sort of nervous. As if

61

the houses might all slide together like houses on a tilted Monopoly board, and fall off the edge.

Leaves trickled down from the spindly dogwood trees like red tears. On someone's front lawn a baby in a playpen had thrown all its toys out onto the grass and lay on its side, too bundled up to move, crying as if its heart would break. Probably its mother had disappeared. Slipped off the edge, and was never coming back.

Jean's arms prickled with gooseflesh, and she rubbed them and scowled. Idiot. She had lived here for nearly two years, and it was perfectly safe, and glittering brightly now under the slanted fall sun.

And she had found a place for Hopscotch, at least for a little while. Hopscotch was happy and safe in a real field, and what more could she possibly want?

"This is my street," she said. "Maryellen Lane."

"How can you tell?" asked Mrs. Remington curiously, as if she really wanted to know.

"By the house on the corner. They have checked curtains in the kitchen window."

"Ah. Of course."

At 10007, Jean got out. "Thank you, I think I know the way now. Can I come and ride Hopscotch tomorrow? I mean, I don't want to be a nuisance, but she's used to being ridden. I can borrow my brother's bike."

"Hopscotch?" said Mrs. Remington, puzzled. "Oh, certainly. Come any time. Any time soon, I mean. Before the shopping center gets there." The jeep jerked convulsively, died, started again, and bounded away bucking.

The clothesline pen was empty. Its gate ties hung dangling. No one trotted up to search her for carrots.

Jean went into the house and upstairs, crawled into her unmade bed with her clothes on, and went to sleep.

When she woke up, it felt late. There were noises downstairs. She scrambled out of bed feeling chilly and confused, the way she always did after naps.

Outside the window it was dusk already. All up and down Maryellen Lane men were standing leaning on their leaf rakes, burning tiny piles of dogwood leaves in the gutters. They stood beside them and watched the low smoke curl and fume, and the sharp sorrowful smell of it hung over the houses. It looked like a kind of dance, Jean thought, or something religious. All the men. All the little piles of smoke.

In the Monroes' yard, the dogwood leaves lay where they had fallen at the feet of the little trees. In Hopscotch's pen the ground was bare except for the scattered hay of her breakfast, and a single heap of poop.

Jean slammed her window and went downstairs. Donald was in the kitchen, stirring macaroni, wreathed in steam. He stirred slowly and rhythmically, with a book open on the stove beside him.

Jean went to get the cheese and the grater.

"Hello," said Donald, pulling his eyes away from the book. "The S.P.C.A. came."

"Oh," said Jean. "What did they say?"

"They wanted to see your pony. I told 'em you'd taken it away to keep it in a stable somewhere, and they said okay."

"You did? But I did! I mean, that's where I was, I found a place for her. Not a stable, but a huge field with a lot of other ponies. It's kind of a farm, or it used to be. Imagine, and it's only two or three miles from here, and we never knew it even existed." Jean grated cheese vigorously, and scraped her knuckle.

"I figured you'd manage something."

"Thanks," she said, blotting up the blood with a napkin.

"For telling them. The S.P.C.A." It seemed years since the morning, with Hopscotch tied to the laundry tub and the whole family screaming.

"I had to tell them something," said Donald reasonably. "They wanted to know." He bent over the book again, a thin, tough-looking little book called *Number Theory,* and turned a page with his left hand, stirring with his right.

That was the thing about families, Jean thought. If you have a fight with them, or hate them, and everyone's miserable, you can't really get *away* from them. They're all still right there, and after a while something nice happens and it's all right again. With friends, you get mad, or say you'll never speak to them again, and you never do. Because in order to get un-mad, you'd have to phone them and say you're sorry, or something. You can lose friends, really lose them, but your family just hangs around so long you aren't mad any more.

"I'm starved," she said. "I didn't have any lunch. Where's Mother?"

"Went to see Mr. Wilcox," Donald mumbled. "Pay for the pool thing. Where'd I put the strainer? Out of the way, you'll get boiled." Steam came ballooning out of the sink. Donald shook the macaroni in the strainer with a steady, circular motion, still reading.

Jean opened the window to let the steam out, and the sad, suburban smell of leaf smoke floated in. Over in her own kitchen, Mrs. Wilcox was moving back and forth getting dinner, and for a moment she and Jean faced each other, separated by the strip of faded grass. She must be thinking, "Hah!" Jean thought.

She turned away, and scraped a blob of butter into the saucepan. "Donald?" she asked cautiously. "Do you hate it here? Here in Dogwood Estates, I mean?"

Donald looked up from his book with difficulty, and gazed remotely at her. He looked a little puzzled, and far away. It was hard to imagine him hating anything, and Jean felt silly asking; she never much talked to Donald about things like that; but he said, "Hate it here? Sure, I hate it here. Who wouldn't?"

They looked at each other for a minute, like strangers wondering if maybe they knew each other from somewhere, and then he said, "Your butter's burning," and went back to his book.

8

In the morning, Jean went out to the empty pen and began to unwrap the clothesline, winding it around her wrist.

Mr. Reece, on his way to the 8:22, stopped his car to roll down the window and call out, "Better tell your mom to get some grass seed in there right away."

Jean always felt a little muddled in the morning. Grass seed? "Why?" she asked.

Mr. Reece scowled. "*Why?* Why, because it's October already. Should have been in the ground a month ago." Jean went on winding up clothesline, and he added, "Don't forget to tell her. This place's been an eyesore long enough. It's high time you people had a little consideration for the rest of us."

He drove away, and Jean watched him turn down Wisteria, and then she coiled up the hose and put it in the garage, and carried the bucket in, and found the hoof-pick, trampled in the dirt, and stuck it in her pocket. There was no more pony pen at 10007. Only the bare patch, and the pole from Shelley's badminton set. She had fifteen minutes before the bus.

Inside, she found a piece of paper and took a pen from her hatband and, carefully slanting her handwriting backward, she wrote, "Please excuse Jean's absence yesterday. I kept her home with a sore throat. Sincerely, Margaret A. Monroe." She put it in her notebook and shouldered the badminton pole and went over to Shelley's.

The Wolframs' kitchen, except for being at the other end of the house, was the same as the Monroes', only cleaner, and yellow instead of avocado; yellow refrigerator, yellow counter tops and stove and oven, yellow dishwasher. Mrs. Wolfram even had yellow curtains at the window. Also, where the Monroes had a pencil drawing of a luna moth the Wolframs had a clock.

The twins were eating Pop Tarts, with jelly on their cheeks. Mrs. Wolfram offered Jean a piece of toast. It was kind of insulting, the way Mrs. Wolfram seemed to think Jean never got meals because her mother worked.

"No, thank you. I had breakfast."

"What did you eat?"

None of your business, thought Jean. "Macaroni and cheese."

"For *breakfast*?"

"There was some left over. We always eat the leftovers for breakfast."

"I never heard of such a thing. Cold macaroni and cheese for breakfast, for heaven's sake. Here, let me just make you a Pop Tart, it won't take a minute, and you can take it with you. You need something hot in your stomach."

"Oh, Mom," said Shelley. "Stop it, we haven't got *time*. Come on, Jean, just stick the pole in the corner. Mom'll put it away. Let's go."

"Macaroni and cheese for *breakfast*," said Mrs. Wolfram.

Outside, the wind whipped Shelley's long hair across her mouth, and Jean had to hold on to her hat. "Where were you yesterday?" asked Shelley. "What did you do with Hopscotch?"

It took Jean all the way to the bus stop, and until the bus got there, to tell the whole story, starting with the Wilcoxes' pool, and Shelley dancing with impatience, crying, "Yes, but where *is* she?" Shelley never wanted to hear the whole story. She liked to know the ending first, and work backwards.

"So she's safe, anyway," she said, settling into a seat across the aisle from Jean. "Everything's okay."

"Not really. The thing is, Mrs. Remington can't pay her taxes, and she's going to have to sell her place to be a shopping center. Then I'm right back where I started from. Hopscotch has no place to live, and Mrs. Remington doesn't either."

"I wonder what kind of stores they'll have," said Shelley. "The shopping center. I hope they have a Strawbridge's. I saw the neatest coat in a Strawbridge ad. Mom said I've got a coat already, but I bet if I asked Dad—"

"But *Shelley*. We have to stop them. We don't *need* another shopping center. And I do need a place for Hopscotch, and Mrs. Remington needs her house. I mean, she's not the kind of lady that could live in an apartment, or Dogwood Estates, they'd laugh at her. We've got to stop them buying it."

"Don't be silly," said Shelley. "You can't *stop* things like that."

"Why not?"

Shelley looked at her, and said slowly, "You know what's the trouble with you, Jean? The trouble with you is, you think you can do everything in the world. And you've got another think coming. That's what." And she turned her shoulder on Jean to talk to Kim Alexander instead.

In history, Jean sat daydreaming through the first gunfire of the Revolution. Highmeadow's sloping fields floated over her desk. She remembered the moldy smell of the big kitchen, and the black-eyed susan petals falling in the sink, and down the maple driveway the little stone tenant house under its cherry tree. Bulldozers would come, and all those things would live only in her head, slowly rubbing themselves out with time until maybe nothing was left but a jar of black-eyed susans against a dusty windowpane, and she wouldn't remember where she'd seen it, and then nothing at all.

And where would Hopscotch go, and the other ponies?

"*Jean*. I said, who was Crispus Attucks?"

Jean opened her mouth to speak, and closed it again, and then said, hopefully, "A British general?" The class laughed.

Bulldozers groaned and rumbled, and the barn toppled and fell slowly in a smoking heap of boards and stones. Ponies wheeled and scattered in panic.

After history, they had library. In the school library, about half the books were new, and bought by the librarian from an approved list, and those were all about careers, or the lives of famous athletes, or kids who took drugs and then were sorry afterward. The rest of the books were donations, things people gave away because they didn't want them anymore. Some of these were pretty interesting.

Jean was reading a book called *Equine Diseases Illustrated,* and wondering if Hopscotch might get swamp fever. Shelley was struggling through something called *Jude the Obscure*. She said she didn't understand much of it, but she was sure it was dirty, or was going to be if she kept at it.

The pages of *Equine Diseases* were brown-speckled with mildew, and tended to crack and flake off at the corners. The room was quiet, rustling only with a sigh, or a muffled giggle, and then the librarian's cross *"Sssh!"* from her desk, where she sat making little piles of cards. Beth Parker sucked on the ends of her hair.

The door opened, and a girl bustled in importantly and gave the librarian a note. She read it, and nodded, and looked vaguely around the room. Her eye stopped on Jean. She crooked her finger.

Jean left *Equine Diseases* opened at the page on thrush, and went over to the desk. "Jean Monroe? You're wanted in the principal's office," said the librarian disapprovingly.

"What for?" She looked from the librarian to the girl who'd brought the message. The girl shrugged. It was not her business to talk to criminals. "I'm sure I don't know," said the librarian, and went back to her cards.

Jean, her chest tight with panic, walked with the messenger girl through the empty halls that smelled of dust, and their feet clacked and echoed. They passed through patches of sound from classrooms, past a teacher saying, ". . . verb in that sentence? Doesn't anyone know?," and the choir room where the sugar-sweet voices of the choir were singing, "To ask the Lord's blessing, He chastens and hastens, His will to make known."

The principal's office had a bench outside the door, in the main office, for bad kids to wait on. Jean sat down.

The minute hand of the clock moved in stiff, palsied jerks. A woman was puttering around the office, one of the women who answered the phone and filed things, and Jean smiled at her, but she folded in her mouth and turned away.

The hall door was open. Anyone passing by could look in and see Jean sitting there, outside Mrs. Mueller's office. No one did, though.

She scrunched down a little and put her thumbs in her pockets and looked at the ceiling, hoping to look casual. Hoping to look as if she'd been called down for some quite ordinary thing, a mistake in the records, or what was her mother's office phone number, or something like that.

Eight minutes jerked by on the clock.

The door to the principal's office opened. "Jean Monroe?"

Her stomach gave a sort of clutching pain, and she went in and sat down in the chair across from Mrs. Mueller's desk.

Mrs. Mueller sat down at her desk. She unfolded a piece of paper and read it through to herself, slowly. She must have read it several times.

Jean could feel sweat creeping down her ribs, cold and tickly. Over the desk was a copy of the Declaration of Independence, and on the wall beside her was a brownish print called "Snowbound" with some framed certificates around it.

Mrs. Mueller passed the paper across to Jean. "Your teacher sent me this," she said. "She said it was clearly not your handwriting, but it didn't seem to be the handwriting of any other human being, either. Now," she held up her hand, "I don't want to hear your version of the story. I don't want to hear any interesting fictions about how your mother broke both arms, and had to dictate your absence excuse to her dog to write, or any other ingenious inventions. I'm taking it for granted that you had something important to do yesterday."

Jean opened her mouth.

"No," said Mrs. Mueller. "I don't want to know about it. I am, naturally, assuming that it will never happen again."

Jean scrumpled the note in her sweaty hand and nodded dumbly.

"The other thing I wanted to talk about . . ." Mrs. Mueller looked thoughtfully at Jean with her head on one side, like someone considering upholstery samples, ". . . is your hat."

"Oh." Jean reached up and put her hand on it.

"Yes. That hat. Your teacher tells me you have been asked politely not to wear it to school, but you continue to do so. She finds it very unpleasant, and to tell you the truth, I do myself. It is not attractive. Do you, perhaps, have some reason for wearing it that you would care to tell me about?"

Her eyes are like green marbles, thought Jean, but she couldn't look away from them. Green marbles rolling around. Slowly, without shifting her eyes from Mrs. Mueller's, Jean took hold of the brim of her hat and pulled it sideways until it slipped off her head.

"I see," said Mrs. Mueller, nodding her head several times. "Is that something you did to *yourself*, Jean?"

"Yes."

"Why?"

"I didn't like the other. It was just . . ." she cleared her throat, ". . . just ordinary."

"So you dyed it. Or tried to. To make it look different."

"Yes."

"And now you wear the hat to hide it. Or perhaps to make yourself look even more different. So you won't get lost in the crowd?"

Jean managed to break her eyes away and look down at her lap and the damp, crumpled note.

"Is that it, Jean?"

Yes, maybe, she thought. Being just like everyone else is the same as being no one at all. Disappearing. Invisible.

"I would like to suggest that there are other ways of standing out from the crowd. You're a capable girl. You might try making better grades than anyone else, for instance. I'm sure you could do it if you put your mind to it."

Jean nodded politely and lost interest. Her eyes slid out of focus until she saw a double blur sitting behind a double desk. The voice went on, and beyond it she could see Highmeadow and its fields and barn, with the shadow of the shopping center creeping across them. Capable. If she put her mind to it. . . .

It came like a new picture bursting over the one in her mind.

Of course. She would have a horse show, and raise the money for Mrs. Remington's taxes. The picture sharpened and brightened and she could see it clearly, spread out like a flag across the field; white fences, crowds cheering, elegant horses with their tails wrapped and their manes braided sweeping around over jumps, hundreds of cars and vans, and everyone hurrying back and forth in gleaming boots in the sunshine.

She would have a horse show. She could hardly wait to get started. She squirmed in her chair.

Mrs. Mueller was saying, ". . . not trying to forbid you to make a spectacle of yourself, you understand. Within reason. If that's what you really want. I'm just asking you to think it over."

"Yes," said Jean. "I mean, thank you." She looked imploringly at the door, and Mrs. Mueller stood up.

"In the meantime," she said, "you may continue to wear that hat, although I certainly think a pretty scarf would make a better choice."

"Thank you," said Jean again, and jammed the hat down securely over her ears as she left.

A horse show. She'd have to get a book on judging,

maybe the school library had one, maybe someone had donated one. Then she'd have to print up notices. No, first she'd better tell Mrs. Remington. Then set up the jumps and make out a list of classes.

In her mind the picture grew clearer and the crowd swelled until it overflowed onto the outside course, where hunters were warming up. Fathers had little kids spraddling their necks for a better view. And among all the polished horses, Hopscotch trotted and tossed her head to flutter the blue ribbon on her bridle. Small Pony Handy Hunter, maybe, 13.2 and under.

She walked slowly back through the empty halls to the library with her head down, watching her feet move. The children's classes always came first. Lead line. Walk, trot. Then walk, trot, canter, and then two-foot jumps for ponies under 13 hands.

Donald could collect the money at the gate. There would certainly be enough for the taxes. Probably enough left over to fix the barn.

She could hardly wait to begin.

9

Mrs. Remington sighed and looked out through the dusty window. On the windowsill, the black-eyed susans had been replaced by a tired chrysanthemum with its neck bent over.

"It seems like such a lot of work," she said. "And where would they all park their cars?"

"Well, there's the drive," said Jean. "And maybe nobody would mind if they parked along the road, sort of in the ditch. Of course the horse vans would have to come onto the field."

"They'll trample the grass dreadfully. I do hope it won't be wet." Mrs. Remington pushed a chunk of gray hair off her forehead, and it fell back down again. "It certainly is nice of you to think of it, Jane. I just don't know, though. Even if I could pay the taxes now, what about next year?"

"We could have it again. An annual horse show, every year. They always do."

"Do you think so? Well, maybe you're right. I said you were a lucky person, didn't I?"

The cat Cleo walked across the kitchen waving her matted tail and stood by the door, staring earnestly up at the door handle. Mrs. Remington opened the door for her, and then absentmindedly followed her outside as if she had forgotten about Jean.

Jean sat waiting for a minute, and then got up and went out after her.

Beyond the kitchen was a square garden, or what used to be one, knee-high in weeds, surrounded by a low stone wall. Brick paths drew an X across it, with the bricks all heaved crooked and soft with moss. Mrs. Remington sat down on the stone wall with her knees apart under the blue dress. "Look at that pesky chickweed," she said. "And the ragweed. Nothing but weeds. This used to be the herb garden, you know. My husband's grandmother started it. Thyme, and sage, and all those things. More for medicine, of course, than flavorings in those days. Not much left but the mint, and that's run wild all over."

"You could pull up the weeds," said Jean.

"Oh, they'd only come back again, you know. It's the way with weeds."

"Is it all right, then?" asked Jean impatiently. "The show? You don't mind?"

"Show? Oh, gracious, child, I don't mind." A yellow leaf blew into her lap, and she picked it up and let the wind take it away again. "It's sweet of you to try to help. It's just that once your luck starts running downhill, it's hard to stop it. It just keeps running till it's all gone."

"I'd better get started, then," said Jean. "On the jumps and stuff."

"I'm sorry there's nothing I can do to help."

"I thought you might be the judge."

"Dear me. I'm afraid I don't know anything about it. It's quite scientific, I'm sure."

"Oh, it's easy," said Jean firmly. "I got a book about it

you can read, I'll bring it tomorrow. Is it okay if I look around in the barn? For stuff to make jumps out of?"

"Certainly, child. Look anywhere you want."

The barn was a treasury of broken furniture and rusted farm machinery and cartons of mildewed books, stacks of old newspapers and empty paint cans and harness and sacks of nails, and even a pony cart that would do for Hopscotch if she could find the missing wheel, but there wasn't much that looked like proper jumps. Not that there was anything *wrong* with jumping over seatless chairs and three-legged tables, but it didn't look professional. She dragged out some bales of hay and stacked them, for one jump, and made a fence of paint cans for another, but she'd have to use branches and brush and fence rails for the rest. The trouble with piled-up jumps like that is they're hard to measure, and besides, they scatter all over when somebody knocks them.

She worked until it was almost dark, and had to pedal home furiously, Donald's ancient bike creaking in protest.

After dinner, she dashed carelessly through her homework and settled down to work on her program, copying the right words from the class list of a show she'd been to last spring.

Maiden Hunter Championship and Reserve.
To be awarded to two of the four horses which have acquired the most points over fences.
Green Hunter—over the outside course, weather permitting, 3'3".
Open Jumper—in the ring, over 8 fences starting at 3'3".
Pony Handy Hunter—shown over a special course, emphasis on manners and promptness.
Open to ponies 13.2 and under.

That was Hopscotch, just barely.

"Goodness, Jeannie, what a lot of homework." Her mother had come prowling into the living room looking for the evening paper.

"It's not, it's my horse show. Look, Mother, can you take this to work and make some copies on the duplicator, if I print it up neatly?"

"Sure. How many do you need?"

"I don't know. I want to put them up all over the place, in the shopping center and the post office and everywhere they'll let me. Then we'll need some more for the show."

"You're going to give them out to everybody?"

Jean considered, rolling the corner of the paper. "That would have to be hundreds, wouldn't it?"

"I can't, lamb. It would take all day. Why don't you just have a few at the show, stuck around in places where people can go look at them?"

"I guess I'll have to."

Donald shambled through on his way to the phone, to call Barry with a chess move. "What makes you think hundreds of people are going to show up?"

"People always come to a horse show," said Jean. "Remember the one we went to last spring? It was mobbed."

"That was a real one," said Donald.

"This is a real one," said Jean. "You're going to collect the money at the gate, okay?"

"Okay, if I have to. What're you charging to get in?"

"I think a dollar-fifty, and seventy-five cents for kids. Entries are five dollars a class."

"That seems like a lot," said her mother.

"We have to make a lot of money. Besides, that's what they charged at the one last spring."

"That was a real one," said Donald again, darkly, and picked up the phone, considering the scrap of paper in his hand. "R to K4," he said to himself. "I think I've got him this time."

"It's about time," said Mrs. Monroe. "Or is this a new game? I can't find the front page, has anyone seen it?"

Jean printed her program up as neatly as possible. It would have looked better done by a proper printer, but she decorated the margins with drawings of horses and horse-shoes, and it didn't look too bad. Unfortunately the copies her mother brought home were sort of dark and smudgy, and it was hard to tell what the horseshoes were. Donald said they looked like cat footprints.

Her mother drove her around with her sheaf of papers and handful of thumbtacks, and they let her put up notices at the post office, and the Sewing Circle and the Drug Fair in the shopping center, and the A & P.

She put one on the bulletin board at school.

Shelley read over her shoulder. "First Annual High-meadow Horse Show. That *sounds* fancy, anyway."

"Sounds okay to me," said Jean. "Listen, you can ride Hopscotch in Class 3 if you want. The walk, trot, canter. You wouldn't have to jump."

Shelley looked away, down the long hall swarming with kids, and frowned vaguely. "I guess not."

"Why not? You could go in the walk, trot, but you'd feel silly. That'll be all really little kids."

"No, thanks."

"Well, if you don't want to. But don't forget to *come*. And bring your mother and the twins. And your father, too, if he wants."

"Oh, I don't know," said Shelley uncomfortably. She scratched with her thumbnail in the doodled brown paper cover of her English book. "I think we're busy next Satur-day. Listen, I've got to go, the bell's going to ring in a minute."

Jean grabbed her sleeve. "Hey. Wait. What's the matter? You can't not *come*. What's the matter with you anymore, anyway, Shell? Are you mad or something?"

Shelley shifted her books uneasily to the other arm, and said, "Nothing. I'm not mad. It's just. . . ." She looked helplessly at her friend. "Oh, Jean, it's just that everybody thinks you're kind of . . . you know. Weird. Like a freak. I can't explain it. With your hat, and everything. They kid me about you."

"For Pete's *sake*!" Jean stamped her foot. "That's the dumbest thing I ever heard. You can't listen to *them*."

Shelley looked embarrassed, and mulish. "Well, I can. My mother thinks so, too. It's not so dumb. You're always doing things, stuff nobody else would think of, like having a pony, and the time you said you could drive your mother's car and it went backwards and smashed the Reeces' barbecue grill. And all those eggs you bought, to hatch into chickens, remember how they stunk? And that strike, or revolution, or whatever you called it, at camp, when you got all the kids together?"

"Well, it worked, didn't it? The food *did* get better, sort of."

"Yes, but that's not what I *mean*. You're always thinking you can do weird things like that, that nobody else does. Thinking you can just put up some signs and have a horse show."

"Why can't I?"

"Because you *can't*. You have to be grown up. Kids can't do things like that. And thinking you can stop a whole shopping center. I'm not mad or anything, but sometimes I think they're right, that's all, and you *are* weird. Listen, there's the bell." She pulled her arm away from Jean and turned and ran clumsily down the hall with her books flapping in her arms and her long hair bouncing from side to side.

Jean stared at the bulletin board, and her horse show notice blurred and shifted through tears. Shelley had been her friend ever since they'd moved to Dogwood Estates from their old apartment. They had made Indian tepees and caves together in the woods, and been the only two members of half-a-dozen secret clubs.

She stretched her eyes wide to keep the tears from spilling.

On the other hand, when the show was a success, and she did pay the taxes and stop the shopping center, Shelley would feel silly. They'd all feel silly.

She looked around to be sure no one was watching before she wiped her eyes on her sleeve, and then broke into a run herself, and skidded into her classroom just as the teacher was saying, "Put your books away, please, and pass the papers back; we're going to have a short quiz."

After school, and all weekend, and half the next week, she pedaled quickly through the flat streets of Dogwood Estates, and along the broken, potholed length of Township Line Road, and down the short stretch of road in front of Highmeadow, and turned into the maple-lined drive and dropped Donald's bike in the weeds in front of the little stone house. She gave Hopscotch a carrot across the billowy honeysuckle fence and went to work.

The outside course had to be all brush jumps. In the ring, the jumps were made up of various things, like an obstacle course. She had found a stack of bean poles in the barn, and those were good propped on paint cans, pieced out with a wooden stepladder missing two rungs and some cartons from which she had unpacked mountains of mildewed books. She found a chair with a torn cane seat for Donald to sit on collecting money. She pinned the programs on the maple trees along the drive. She lettered signs with arrows on them, saying PARKING and ALL VANS THIS WAY, and ENTRANCE, for the ring, because there wasn't any fence around it even to show where the ring was.

She printed a stack of numbers up to a hundred for riders, and cut a whole bagful of ribbons out of construction paper and lettered each one FIRST ANNUAL HIGH-MEADOW HORSE SHOW. It took hours.

Some of the jumps were balanced precariously, and the bay pony enjoyed pulling them down. Patiently Jean walked around the course setting them up again, and the ponies followed, pleased at all the activity, discussing it with little kicks and squeals.

By Wednesday it was as finished as it was going to be. Jean stood back and squinted at it.

It was a shame there was no real ring, with a fence. There wasn't even a worn track to show the way to go. Well, tomorrow she would take Hopscotch around a few times, maybe that would wear it down some.

A couple of the brush jumps were terribly crooked.

Jean sucked a splinter in the ball of her thumb. It didn't really look right. It looked a lot like scattered piles of junk. Like what was left after a garage sale.

Of course, when people were there, standing around the ring, and horses, and vans parked all over, it would look better. More like a horse show.

She squinted her eyes narrowly, and concentrated hard, imagining. Gradually the paint cans and cartons faded, and she saw it all again, flags snapping in the wind, white fences, horses burnished and braided, whinnying, and the great crowd of people. She could hear them hold their breath before a high jump, and then the long *"Aah!"* of relief as he made it, or the down-falling *"Ooh"* if he didn't, and the jump crew running out to replace the bar. Dogs, children, lunch boxes, people rushing busily around, carrying saddles, carrying Cokes, tying on their numbers. And always some show-off with a pony cart trotting back and forth and getting in the way.

She felt better, and turned her back on the glittery scene and went to get Donald's bike.

At the foot of the drive the little stone house looked down at her with its empty windows of wavery glass. Now it had a broken chair in the front yard for Donald to sit on, and that made it look even more abandoned, like a place where people dumped things.

She dropped the bike and kicked through the long grass to peer in a window, on tiptoe.

The window was dusty and vines had grown across it, but she could see a long room with a floor of wide boards, and a lot of junk. Scraps of lumber, boxes, a bedspring propped against the wall. The same sort of junk the barn was full of.

She backed away and looked up. It was a very personal kind of house, she thought. It had a face, of course, as all houses have faces, made of doors and windows, but there was something particularly good about this one's. If it had been a person, it would be a nice person, she thought. Quiet and friendly. But sad, with the branches of the big cherry tree scratching back and forth on its shingle roof to make an empty noise.

She picked the bike out of the weeds again and started home.

Tomorrow she would start schooling Hopscotch for the show. She'd have to work her hard; there wasn't much time, and she hadn't even been ridden for a week. Friday she would wash her and shampoo her tail and brush her for an hour. Saturday was the show.

10

Mrs. Remington's ponies watched with interest while Hopscotch circled over the fences. She was misbehaving, showing off for her new friends, and kept throwing her head up and dancing sideways at the jumps. Jean wrestled with her until she was exhausted and they were both wet. Then she rubbed her down and turned her loose with the others, who clustered around to nose her jealously.

Jean felt a little jealous herself. After all, there had been a time when she was Hopscotch's only friend. A time when Hopscotch nickered sorrowfully after her when she went to catch the school bus, and watched her out of sight, ears sharp with anxiety. Still, it was such a relief to know she was happy, and safe. Safe for a time, and maybe forever.

The next day, Friday, she took her out by the gate and up to the big house, and washed her with the hose and a bucket and an old broom from the barn. She washed the long straw-colored tail with her own shampoo, and spent twenty minutes picking burrs.

It wasn't a warm day. It was cloudy, with a damp wind blowing, and Jean walked her till her feet hurt, trying to dry her off, and rubbed her hard with her sweater. She was beginning to get her winter coat in, thick and fleecy and impossible to dry.

Jean put her back in the field, and Hopscotch trotted a few steps and then folded her knees and rolled. Back and forth she scratched herself luxuriously in the thin grass, and then stood up and shook herself in a cloud of dust, satisfied and streaked with dirt.

Tomorrow Jean would give her a good brushing, early, and tie her somewhere to keep her clean.

Now for the tack.

She took a flat can of saddle soap from her pocket and examined the bridle.

The reins were tied together lumpily in two places, making them so short that when Hopscotch dropped her head Jean almost tumbled down her neck. Even cleaned, and the bit polished, that wasn't going to look very elegant.

And there was no saddle at all.

Jean stared gloomily at the fact, hanging in the air in front of her.

She was so used to having no saddle that she had managed to forget it, but how could you ride bareback in a show? It wasn't professional. No one did, unless it was a kind of kiddies' show, with bareback classes and a barrel race. This wasn't that kind of show.

She had seen a saddle in the barn, up in the loft, but it was a Western saddle, cracked and mildewy, with no stirrups. Even if it had stirrups, you couldn't ride Western in a jumping class. It wasn't a rodeo.

Soberly she rubbed saddle soap into her broken reins. It was beginning to seem possible that everything would not be all right. Hopscotch might not be the star of the show. The show itself might not be all right.

She looked out over the field, and the jumps made of hay bales and broken ladders.

Slowly, as always, the field faded out and changed, and she saw the vans and people hurrying, and heard horses neighing to each other, and the loudspeaker saying, "Next entry, please. Next horse into the ring. Number twenty-two in the ring, please."

Of course it would be all right. In her mind she saw a faceless person in breeches carrying a saddle, and she thought, of course, I'll borrow a saddle. With all those horses, there's bound to be a saddle no one's using for that class. I'll borrow one, that's all.

Smiling, she bent back over the bridle again and rubbed the soap into it until it felt soft and expensive under her fingers, and elegant and gleaming, the way it should have been.

The next morning she woke up painfully early, in the dark, and lay and waited for daylight, running over the list of classes in her head. When it was gray enough to see, she got up and dressed and padded downstairs to make a cup of tea.

She was wearing clean pants, and a white shirt, and had even brushed her wrecked hair quickly before she put on her hat. It was a shame she didn't have proper clothes, but maybe there would be other kids, at least in the pony classes, in jeans and sneakers.

She stirred her tea to cool it, and the dim sunless daylight grew in the room. Outside, across the street, the Pikes' burglar lights went off. The Pikes were away. They had a special gadget that turned the lights on and off, so you'd think they were there, but you could always tell when they weren't because they left a folding chair in the front yard, with a magazine and a coffee cup beside it, to fool the burglars. It was there now.

Jean finished her tea before Donald and her mother came straggling in yawning.

"It's going to rain," said Donald.

"Don't say it," said Mrs. Monroe. "Nervous, lamb?"

"No," said Jean. "Yes, I guess so. My stomach hurts."

"Don't try to eat anything." Mrs. Monroe turned on the news. Donald ate leftover spaghetti sauce on a piece of toast. Jean fidgeted impatiently, chewing the bitten skin around her fingernails.

"But it isn't even eight o'clock yet," said her mother.

"I have to brush her. I have to catch the other ponies and tie them up. There's so much to *do*."

"Oh, all right. All right. Come on, Donald."

They drove through Dogwood Estates as it woke up slowly into the gray day, the houses still looking blank and dead, and only a few men up already and washing their cars in their driveways.

At Highmeadow they parked around behind the barn, where the vine-covered truck sat decaying in a twitter of birds, to be out of the way of the other cars. The dogs came roaring up, barking and wagging their tails until Jean clapped her hands and they slunk away.

The air was raw and chilly. Dark billows of clouds bulged down low over the field.

"What a beautiful, beautiful place," said Mrs. Monroe. "Imagine you finding it, Jeannie, hidden away like this. There's Route 9 right down there, and I never saw the house here, even in winter."

"Where do I sit?" asked Donald.

"Down by the road, by the little stone house. What did you bring a book for? You won't have time to read."

They walked down the deep curve of the drive with gold maple leaves falling all around them through the gray air. Hopscotch whinnied and followed them along the fence.

In front of the little house, Donald dusted leaves off his broken chair, and said, "Who lives here?"

"Nobody," said Jean. "There's no plumbing."

"Oh. Nice, though." He opened his book, which was called *Computer Analysis of Data,* and slumped into his usual position with his chin in his left hand and his left elbow on his right wrist.

Jean caught Hopscotch, and her mother helped brush her and pick the new burrs out of her forelock. "I bet you're the prettiest pony in the show, anyway," she said. Hopscotch pawed with her little forefoot and looked modestly away, across the field, under her blond eyelashes. "I should have pulled her mane," said Jean, "so I could braid it. I just didn't have time."

"She looks lovely," said her mother. Hopscotch gave her an affectionate push with her nose that made her stagger. Mrs. Monroe rubbed the furry ears. "I hope," she said, a little dubiously, "that everything's going to work out all right, lamb. With your show."

"Of course it will." But her stomach still felt odd, as if it might know something she didn't.

The dog chorus broke out again, and Mrs. Remington came out of the big house and walked across the field toward them in a cloud of leaping dogs. From far away, she looked like a doll, a dumpy, trudging, little doll in a blue dress. She was puffing slightly as she came up to them.

Jean introduced her mother, and said, "Did you finish reading that book?"

"Not exactly. I brought it with me." Mrs. Remington pushed her glasses up securely on her little nose and held the book out at arm's length, examining its cover. It was called *Elements of Judging and Showing*, and it was really pretty dull. "I'm afraid I was never much interested in showing. My husband hunted, of course, so much more exciting, I always thought. The pink coats, you know. Silver flasks."

Mrs. Monroe had picked a milkweed pod, and the wind was tearing little silky tatters off it. "You must have lots of monarchs here," she said.

"I beg your pardon?"

"In the summer. Monarch butterflies. Their larvae eat milkweed leaves."

Mrs. Remington looked polite.

Mrs. Monroe tossed the milkweed away, and said, "I love your house. How old is it?"

For the first time, Mrs. Remington brightened with intelligence. "Ah," she said. "The main section there is relatively new, 1877, but the wing, where the kitchen is, that's the original, what's left of it. Would you like to come in? Perhaps a glass of sherry. . . ."

"I'd love to."

The two women moved off down the hill with the dogs following, and Mrs. Remington saying, "Some of Washington's officers were quartered there. So destructive. My husband's people were Loyalists, of course. . . ."

Jean stood holding her pony on the windy hillside and waited. Her nose started to run. Down below her, Donald sat in the front yard of the little house, reading, with a shoe box at his feet for making change. She wondered what time it was. Mrs. Remington's ponies, tied to the fence, ate the withered honeysuckle leaves.

The ENTRANCE sign by the first jump had blown over. She propped it up again with stones.

For warmth, she scrambled up on Hopscotch and trotted aimlessly back and forth, wishing she had a watch. People should be coming soon, with their vans. She squinted up the road. The first class was for nine o'clock.

After forever, the two women came out of the big house

again and started across the field, Mrs. Remington carrying a glass and chatting up at Mrs. Monroe like a cheerful child. Jean cantered over.

"Where is everyone?" asked Mrs. Monroe. "It's past nine."

Past nine.

The field was empty except for her mother and Mrs. Remington and herself on the pony. The wind blew damp and hateful. Her jumps looked suddenly fragile and rickety, nothing but heaps of junk.

The little road was empty of vans, even of cars. No one had driven by since they came. Was everyone lost? Should she have put up signs, to show the way?

Then two boys came by on bicycles, and stopped to lean against the fence. Jean kicked Hopscotch into a trot and went over to them.

"This where the horse show's supposed to be?" asked one of them.

"It's seventy-five cents apiece for kids," she said. "You pay over there."

"Seventy-five cents?" he said. "For what?"

"I guess it's a public road," said the other. "We got a right to be on the public road."

Jean stared helplessly at them. Hopscotch tore up some ragweed and chewed on it, roots dangling.

After a while the first one said, "Aw, come on. It's nothing." And they got back on their bikes and pedaled away toward Route 9.

Jean rode slowly back to her mother and Mrs. Remington, who was saying, ". . . a Shaw before I married, and we were Pennsylvanians, of course. *All* the Shaws were Pennsylvanians."

Jean's mother bent over with her back to the wind, trying to light a cigarette. The matches kept blowing out.

90

If only someone would come, Jean thought, just one person, one van, one horse. If only *someone* would come.

And then she thought, no. That would be worse.

You cannot have a show with one horse and one saddleless pony. If someone came, she would have to explain, explain to someone who'd been up half the night wrapping a tail, maybe, and then wrestling the horse into a van. Explain that there wasn't any show. It was all in her mind.

Please, God, don't let anyone come.

No one did.

At twenty after ten it started to rain. Mrs. Monroe and Mrs. Remington went back in the house to drink sherry and Donald went to sit in the car behind the barn with his book.

Yellow leaves ripped off the maple trees in swirls. The sign that said ALL VANS THIS WAY got soggy and pulled off its pin and blew away into the stream, where it floated messily.

Rain dribbled off the edges of Jean's hat and down her neck. Her picture of the horse show, with its glitter and flags and white fences, turned to fog and faded away. In its place, the bulldozers came, and knocked down the sagging barn and the little stone house. Steamrollers smoothed out acres and acres of black parking lot across the ponies' grass.

She blinked it away, and looked stonily at the real fields and the cold, hopeless rain. With stiff fingers she took Hopscotch's polished bridle off and untied the other ponies from the fence, and they moved off, warm in their thick coats, cropping weeds in the rain.

Shelley was right. She was crazy. She was helpless, there was nothing she could do, she was only a child.

No one had come.

11

Donald came downstairs in his pajamas, scratching his hair. "Where's the paper?"

"Mother took it into her room."

He disappeared, and came back with the Hobbies and Recreation section. "You still sulking?"

"I'll sulk if I feel like it."

"Seems dumb. But be my guest." He folded the paper back to the Chess Game of the Week and hunched over it, scowling with concentration.

Jean pulled her hat down low on her forehead and stared out from under it, through the picture window at the day, which was sunny, of course. A lovely day for a horse show. Not that it would have made any difference. She had slept in her clothes, too miserable to undress, and now she was wearing her bathrobe over them, wrapped tightly around her huddled knees.

The phone rang, and then stopped in mid-ring as her mother picked it up in the bedroom. At least her mother wasn't trying to console her. Probably she'd forgotten the horse show already. Nothing was allowed to intrude on Mrs. Monroe's Sunday mornings with the paper. She spent hours with it, consuming it slowly, section by section, like a big orange. She really got her money's worth out of a paper, even carefully reading all the stuff they put in at the bottom to fill out the columns, about how much a blue whale eats, and how many telephones there are in Nigeria.

Jean felt empty and squeezed inside. Maybe she ought to eat something, but nothing she could think of seemed like the right thing to eat.

What an idiot she was. An idiot. An *idiot*. Who around here would come to a horse show? Who had anything to ride except her? And why had she thought she could save Highmeadow from the shopping center, she, Jean Monroe, all alone, like Superman stopping a speeding train with his hand stuck out? Who did she think she was, anyway? There was nothing she could do, and Shelley was right.

Highmeadow was lost. Hopscotch would have no home.

Her stomach tightened, and hurt.

Outside, the bare, trampled pony place was empty in the sunshine. A section of it had been dug up, inexpertly, with her pitchfork, as if someone had been looking for buried treasure.

Yesterday afternoon, Donald had announced that he was going to dig it up and have it ready to plant vegetables there in the spring. It was the perfect place for a vegetable garden, he said, especially since there was no grass there to be wasted. He had gone out after lunch, with his collar turned up against the rain, and started digging, hunched over the pitchfork like a stork.

He hadn't been working ten minutes before Mr. Reece came out of his house with a big black umbrella, and marched across the Wilcoxes' front lawn and up to Donald. From her bedroom window, Jean had watched him talking, waving his free hand, and finally Donald throwing down the pitchfork and coming back inside.

Later, all Donald would say was, "He says you have to plant vegetables in the backyard. Not the front. He says it doesn't look right."

"Vegetables don't look right?" asked Mrs. Monroe, blinking.

And Donald said, "He says it looks like Tobacco Road. Whatever that means."

Now the pitchfork and the partly spaded yard lay abandoned in the sunshine. Inside, Donald scowled over his chess problem.

Jean crossed her hands over her stomach and pressed down, trying to quiet the aching.

Her mother came into the room, barefoot, carrying a coffee cup, and looked at her two children with a slightly confused air, as if she wondered where they came from. "That was Mrs. Pike on the phone," she said.

"More strange noises in the night?" asked Donald, not looking up.

"Not this time. It seems she's just tracked down something called ASTRO. I think that's what she said. It stands for After School Teen Recreational something-or-other. She thought maybe you kids would like to join it."

"No," said Jean. Donald didn't bother to answer.

Mrs. Monroe folded her legs and sat awkwardly on the edge of the coffee table. "It might be interesting," she went on, hopefully. "It meets over in Bedlington every day, and there's a bus that goes straight from your schools. I could pick you up on my way home. They have basketball, and arts and crafts. . . ." Her voice trailed off.

"When would I ride Hopscotch?"

"Why's Mrs. Pike so worried about us, all of a sudden?" asked Donald, tossing the paper on the floor. "I didn't know she cared. She always looks at me as if I was the Boston Strangler."

94

Mrs. Monroe looked embarrassed. "She seems to think you're . . . unsupervised, was the word she used. Apparently she spent Friday night in Newark with her parents, and they told her a lot of grisly stories about teenagers. She says it's not right to have you just hanging around, with no one home."

"What do you mean, no one home? Am I no one?" said Donald indignantly. "Does she think I'm going to rush over and burgle her after school, just because you're at work?"

"Well, as a matter of fact, yes. I think that's just what she thinks."

Donald grinned. "Maybe I will. I bet she'd love it. Just think, all these years she's been getting ready for burglars, and no burglars ever showed up. She just keeps waiting and waiting, poor lady. Yes, I think it would be nice of me to drop in and steal her spoons, one of these days."

"When do we have to start this teen thing?" asked Jean bitterly. "Tomorrow, I suppose?"

"Oh, lamb, you don't have to go if you don't want to."

"Of course we have to," said Jean. "Mother, *you* can't do anything about it. Mrs. Pike'll go around and talk to everyone, and start them all worrying, and calling up, and coming over. Then she'll probably lose some stupid earring or something, and blame it on Donald and me, and the police'll come, and pretty soon we'll just *have* to go. We might as well give up right now. What's the use?"

"You're being hysterical," said her mother. "Mrs. Pike can't *make* you do anything, Jean. Not even all the neighbors coming here complaining all together." But she looked terribly unhappy at the thought.

Donald stood up. "I'm going to get dressed," he said. "Before I get known as the Pajama Burglar. Jean, you going over to your place to clean up?"

"Clean up?" It was horrible to think of going back to

Highmeadow. Unpinning the signs. Dragging the jumps away.

"I'll come give you a hand if you want."

They took turns riding Donald's bike through Dogwood Estates, cold and shiny in the sunlight. Cars that were not washed yesterday were being washed today, and the sun winked and flashed off their fresh polish. Some people were stretching blue winter covers over their round blue swimming pools, and at the backs of some of the driveways basketball nets had been set up and big boys were dribbling and passing to each other. One man was wrapping up his dogwood tree in strips of brown paper, winding them carefully up its skinny trunk like bandaging a horse before a race. Hose water ran along the gutters from the car-washers, gurgling softly.

"I didn't think things could possibly get any more horrible," Jean said. "And then this teen thing came. I guess it just proves it. That things can always get worse."

"Don't go, then," said Donald. "I'm not."

"They'll make us. Don't you see? We're helpless. Look at my horse show. It's stupid to keep fighting, when there's nothing we can do about *anything*."

"My turn," said Donald, and slung his leg over the bike. "Sure you can do things. You just have to tell the real things from the things that aren't real."

"What's that supposed to mean?"

"You're so dumb," said Donald kindly. "Look. Lots of things you can make happen if you work hard enough on it. And if you've got the kind of mad faith you've got." He gave a short laugh, like a bark.

Embarrassed, Jean looked at the ground. It was funny to think of Donald thinking about what she was like. Thinking about her as somebody, not just a sister who was sort of there.

"Other things," he went on, "you can't make happen if you work till you're blue, because they're not real. They're just a dream you had. Something you imagined. Like your horse show."

"How am I supposed to tell the difference?"

Donald shrugged. "That's your worry."

The ponies were grazing among the sad remains of the show, Hopscotch's forelock stiff with burrs again. Carton jumps had crumpled messily in the rain. The stack of numbers from one to a hundred had blown all over, and the bales of hay were wet and spoiled and chewed by ponies. The glittery fall sunshine on everything made it worse. Junkier. Jean and Donald worked silently, trailed by curious ponies and sometimes a dog or two, carrying things back to the barn, dragging the brush jumps back into the woods, gathering up the torn, bleary signs and rider numbers.

"I guess that's everything," said Donald at last.

"The chair," said Jean. "Your chair."

Most of the leaves had blown off the big maples along the drive, and the little stone house stood out sharp and lonely against the blue sky. The chair seat was drifted deep in yellow leaves.

"That's a nice little house," said Donald. "It looks solid. Like it was going to last forever."

"It looks sad," said Jean. "Like it was going to get bull-dozed."

"I bet they have trouble knocking it down. Maybe they won't. Maybe they'll keep it, for a giftie shoppie or something." He put the chair back down and sloshed through leaves and wet grass to the front door.

"It's locked, isn't it?" asked Jean.

"Why would it be locked?" Donald pressed the heavy

iron latch and pulled, and the door swung open, stiffly, groaning. "Come on. Let's look."

It was cold inside. There was an interesting, complicated smell of kerosene and mildew. In between the boxes and junk and stacks of old mail-order catalogs the wide boards of the floor were soft with dust. Donald sneezed. In front of the stone fireplace stood a black iron stove, its stovepipe poked through the wall and a box of rusty nails and hinges on top of it. Jean realized she'd been holding her breath, and let it out in a gasp.

"That stove's how they heated the place," said Donald. He opened the heavy little iron door and they peered in at a drift of white ashes. "Burns wood, I guess. Or coal."

"There's the kitchen," said Jean. They were both whispering.

The kitchen contained an old push-type lawn mower, several cartons of Mason jars, a kitchen table with a rusted iron frying pan and some tin water basins on it, a large white cooking stove and a sink with a little pump behind it.

Jean tried the handle of the pump. A dead wasp fell out of its spout. "It doesn't work."

"I bet it does. Let me." Donald creaked it up and down vigorously, and presently a thin trickle of brownish water drizzled out. He peered down the drain. "Runs right outside," he said. "Waters the flowers. No waste."

"I'm going upstairs."

Upstairs there were two bedrooms, big, empty, shapely rooms, with sun filtering in through their dirty windows onto the bare floors. The east one had faded red roses on its wallpaper, and the west one had little garlands on a faded whitish-blue, swollen and peeling under the windows.

A narrow staircase went on up to the attic. "Hah," said

Donald. "Now, *here's* a room." It ran the whole length of the house, with sharply sloping ceilings and a small low window at each end. "Privacy," he said with satisfaction. "*And* a view."

Jean kneeled on the floor and wiped a clean place on the window. She could see the curve of the hillside, and the barn, and the woods beyond, and blue sky.

"Donald," she began slowly, and stopped.

"Huh?"

"I don't know. Nothing. I guess it isn't real, again, like the show. But I wish we could live here. I mean, nobody's *using* it."

"*Live* here?"

"Yes."

"There's no plumbing. An outhouse. Come on, stupid. We can't live without plumbing."

"People used to. I found a doll's head. . . . *Everyone* used to." She stood up suddenly, and cracked her head on the slanted ceiling. "Ouch. I mean, real people, like us, *everybody*. And right now this minute, thousands of people, I guess millions of people all over the world live without plumbing, don't they?"

"Nobody *I* know."

"Yes, but that doesn't mean we can't. If people can, if everybody did once, then why *can't* we?" She scrubbed at her hat where the lump was rising underneath.

"Okay, well, in theory, we can. It wouldn't kill us. But what about Mother? What about washing clothes, and dishes, and baths?"

"Oh," Jean waved them away impatiently. "You heat water on the stove. Look, there's even a pump in the kitchen. Up there in the woods there's a wreck of an old house where people lived and they had to go down the hill to get water from a spring, and carry it up in a bucket. I bet a pump in the kitchen would've looked pretty good to *them*."

"That's why the place's deserted, they dropped dead from carrying water. Jean, you're goofy. That horse show didn't teach you anything, did it?"

"Sure. It taught me about things being, you know, like you said, real and not real. But I just don't see what's not real about living here. I know it'd be a lot of work. I'm *not* dreaming it's something it isn't." She swiped away a cobweb hanging from her hat, and glared at her brother.

"Okay, say we could live without plumbing. What about the shopping center? You want to live with no plumbing in the middle of a shopping center?"

Jean's mouth came slowly open and stayed that way.

"Forgot about that, didn't you? Didn't you? What are you staring like that for? You look like a goldfish."

"Donald. Listen. If we lived here, if we bought it from Mrs. Remington, or rented it, I guess we'd have to, or whatever, and *paid* her, then that's the money for the taxes, isn't it? I mean, we pay every month on the mortgage at home, don't we? Well, we just give that same money to Mrs. Remington for rent, and she pays the taxes and gets to keep the whole place, the way she should. And I get to keep Hopscotch forever, and you can plant a million vegetables. I mean, just for pumping a little *water*. *Why not?*"

Donald rubbed his hand hard over his chin and the back of his hair, struggling for an answer. "Because you're out of your mind, that's why," he said finally.

"But why *not*?"

"I don't know," he said. He looked at her with his hair standing up in back, and sighed. "I don't know why not. Oh, brother. Here we go again."

12

Mrs. Remington took them into the parlor, which was full of dark, looming, old furniture. Jean sat down cautiously on the edge of an enormous chair in blackish-red plush. It prickled and smelled moldy.

"I finished reading your book on show-judging, Joan," said Mrs. Remington. "Most interesting. Such a pity about your show, wasn't it? But it was fated to happen."

"I'm sorry," said Jean. "It was me. I didn't think. People around here just don't have horses."

"I can't imagine why not. My husband kept three hunters at one point. Dangerous sport, of course. But you mustn't feel bad, Jean. Don't think it was your fault, or that your luck's run out. It's *my* luck, you see. When it's gone, it's simply gone, you know, and there isn't any left." She spread open her stubby little hands to show they were empty, as if luck were something like marbles, or pennies, that you carried around.

"I don't think luck had anything to do with it," said Jean stubbornly. "And it *was* my fault. Just barging ahead without thinking like that."

"I wonder if there might be some sort of curse on the place," said Mrs. Remington thoughtfully. "I must look up curses. I wonder how you tell."

"I hope there isn't," said Donald, "because we've come to ask you about something. At least, Jean has."

Mrs. Remington listened with her head on one side like a sparrow, while Jean explained.

"I must say it would be very nice," she said. "To have the company, you know. And the money, of course. But heavens, it's out of the question."

Jean's heart sank.

"There's no plumbing, you see. No running water."

"We know that," said Donald. "We kind of hoped we could manage without it."

"Oh, no, no, no, no. Your poor mother," said Mrs. Remington. "Such an interesting woman, too. Very intelligent about the Revolution, she quite understands the plight of the Loyalists."

"She's a lepidopterist, actually," said Donald. "I don't think she knows much about history."

"Exactly. Think of her carrying all that water."

"We'd do that, Donald and me," said Jean. "Besides, there's a pump in the kitchen."

"Is there? So there is, I forgot. And the electric, too. We had the electric put in in 1939. Or '40. For that fellow, what was his name?"

"What do you think you would charge for rent?" asked Donald.

"Heavens, child, I don't know. Whatever you think. Or I could ask my lawyers. But what am I saying? I'm sure your poor mother would be horrified. You'd have to talk to her first."

Donald looked at Jean. After all, it was Jean's idea. "I think," she said slowly, "that first we ought to clean it up some. I mean, I don't want it to be like the horse show. If we just drag her over here right off, and show her, with the mess and everything, she might just say no, and once she says no it's sort of hard for her to turn around and say yes. So maybe we better clean it up and make it nice."

"And put in a couple of bathrooms," said Donald.

They worked like dogs. Every afternoon after school they rode Donald's bike over and pitched in, raising billows of dust.

First they had to carry the junk out, and there was a lot of it. Too much to put out for the trash man, and they couldn't just dump it in the yard, so they carried everything up the long drive to the barn and added it to the things in there, where it hardly showed at all. They carried mountains of old magazines and newspapers, and the bedspring, and cartons of empty jars and bottles, and rusty cans, and the lawn mower, and the dusty cracked plates and dishes out of the kitchen cupboards. There was a dead mouse in one cupboard, dried up and withered and light as the shadow of a mouse. Jean took it carefully by the tail and slung it out the kitchen door into the deep grass.

It took them two afternoons just to empty the house. Empty, it looked bigger. It looked cheerier, too. More like a house waiting for some people, and less like a place to keep trash.

"The weird thing is," said Jean, rubbing a streak of dirt into her forehead, "even all dirty and empty like this, it feels more like a *house* than our real house does. It's a *housey* house."

"That's because it was built for somebody to live in," said Donald. "Not like Dogwood Estates, they were built for somebody to sell."

Jean nodded, and washed her hands, one at a time, under the pump's cold rusty water. Funny about Donald, he was

103

getting almost like having a friend. Funny, knowing him all your life, and then having him turn out to be a friend.

They brought the cleaning stuff from home in a knapsack, Windex and Ajax and rags and sponges and ammonia, and Donald shouldering the mop like a rifle.

They did the windows first, to let more light in, cutting the vines away and then washing, Donald on the outside and Jean on the inside.

"Look what you can *see* from here," cried Jean. "There's my Hopscotch. Hi, Hop!" She pushed the swollen old window up with difficulty and whistled piercingly. The pony moved closer to the fence, ears alert, and then saw her, and nickered with pleasure. "Imagine," said Jean. "I can look right out the window and there she is, in a field. *Ow*. The window won't stay up."

"I think you have to prop it with something, like a stick," said Donald. "That's what they did. Listen." They could hear the stream, chuckling and gurgling across the field. "Who says we don't have running water? Imagine going to sleep listening to that instead of the Wilcoxes' television."

"We can build a dam," said Jean, "and have a pond."

They were used to housework, but this was more and harder than they had ever done before. Jean kept falling asleep over her geography. Their shoulders hurt.

They swiped down the dangling curtains of cobweb from the ceiling, and scrubbed the woodwork, and mopped the soft old floors, until everything smelled of cleaning stuff. Then they propped the windows open for air.

The kitchen took two afternoons, cupboard shelves and the stove and the floor, which turned out to be a rather ugly yellowish pattern of linoleum. Donald worked the pump until the water ran clear, and they each solemnly took a drink out of their cupped hands.

"Hey, it's good," said Jean, her chin dripping.

Donald found a scythe in the barn, and cleaned and sharpened it, and they cut the weeds in the yard, inexpertly, nearly chopping off their feet. Finished, it looked more like a homemade haircut than a mowed lawn, but at least, as Jean said, it wasn't as deep.

Last of all, they went out back and inspected the privy.

It sat half-hidden under a great overgrown lilac bush. The door was closed with a hook, and they opened it solemnly and peered inside.

The seat was built up like a bench, and had two oval holes in it. "For company," said Donald. "So you don't get lonesome. The family that. . . . Well. What's in that can?" He opened it. "Powdered sugar?"

"Lime," said Jean. "You use it for horses, too, for stalls. It keeps down the flies, and sort of . . . sweetens things."

Donald sprinkled a handful down through one of the holes, and looked around. "It's not so awful, I guess," he said doubtfully. "I thought it would maybe smell, or something. Okay, let's get to work. Where's the sponge?"

They scraped more cobwebs, and fleets of indignant spiders scattered in all directions. Whitewash flaked off the walls and stuck in their eyelashes and coated Jean's hat like snow. In a corner, where the bench didn't quite meet the wall, they disturbed a squealing family of baby mice, looking like pink erasers, luxuriously nested in toilet-paper shreds. Jean carried them outside wrapped in her sweater and tried to make a new home for them under the lilac. They squeaked frantically.

"Oh dear," she said. "Maybe I ought to bring them back."

"No," said Donald, gathering up the toilet-paper nest and throwing it down one of the holes. "They might just be the last straw. For Mother, I mean. You never know what's going to turn people off."

"Donald?"

"Huh? Hand me that brush."

"Suppose she says no?" Jean looked out through the open privy door, through the bare branches of the cherry tree at the back of the little stone house. Its clean windows reflected sunset, like a house with lights in it where somebody lived. I have to live here, she thought. Was it babyish, a dream, like the horse show? Like pretending to live in a cave or a tepee in the woods? *Could* a person live here? But it wasn't a cave, it was a real house, and real people had lived there before.

"If she says no," said Donald, brushing dust and whitewash toward the doorway, "then we stay in Dogwood Estates. And go to the Teen After School Whatsit and learn to make paper-strip place mats. Mrs. Remington loses Highmeadow. You lose Hopscotch. And we've done all this work for nothing. Move out of the way."

"We could run away," said Jean. "Live here ourselves."

Donald looked up, shocked. "And leave Mother? All alone, with the neighbors? Are you out of your gourd?"

Jean sighed. "She can't say no. She just can't."

"She can too," said Donald grimly.

They carried water out from the kitchen pump in an empty paint can and scrubbed the whole privy. "We ought to put up some pictures," said Jean.

"We ought to have some hot water," said Donald.

They left the door swinging open to dry the soaked wood.

Donald wiggled his shoulders. "I hurt all over," he said. "I guess we're finished. I don't know what more we can do."

Together they stood looking back at the house. Cherry-tree branches scratched on the roof. The reflection of sunset passed off the windows, leaving them empty. A lopsided V of geese flapped overhead, honking like a traffic jam.

"We could put the chicken house over there," said Jean. "By the stream."

"*Chicken* house?" said Donald. "What chicken house?"

"I was thinking we could build one."

Donald snorted. In the eastern sky the first star appeared, suddenly, and twinkled. "Star light," said Jean desperately, "star bright, first star I've seen tonight. . . ."

"You're getting like Mrs. Remington," said Donald in disgust. "If Mother says no, she says no. Stars won't help. Come on, carry some of this stuff. Carry the mop."

They were tired, and the trip through Dogwood Estates seemed like forever. Lights were on. All the picture windows had lights in them, up and down Wisteria Drive. Fathers were coming home, and their cars moved slowly down the streets like a procession, and fell out one at a time as each turned from the line into his own driveway, and the groaning rattle of garage doors passed from house to house like an echo. It was cold. One by one the front doors opened, casting light, and sometimes a smell of cooking came out, or a baby's crying.

"When are you going to tell her?" asked Donald. "Or ask her, or invite her, or whatever?"

"After dinner, I guess," said Jean. "What's tonight? Hot dogs and beans? I'm starved. And Donald. . . ."

"Huh?" Donald was pushing the bike by its handlebars, bent over under the bulging knapsack.

"Should I tell her about it first? Or ask her to come over, and then surprise her?"

He considered as he trudged along, and then said, "It looks better than it sounds. Better show her first. Surprise her."

13

"After you," said Donald gallantly, and Mrs. Monroe went first through the low doorway, peering around as if she expected the surprise to jump out at her.

In her jeans and old sweater, she moved across the room, touching the wood stove, the stones of the fireplace, the long windows. It was a cloudy day, chilly inside, and the gray light came in softly, leaving the corners of the rooms dark.

Jean could feel the little house waiting as fiercely as she was. "Isn't it nice?" she croaked anxiously.

"Nice? Oh, the house? Yes, it's sweet. I can see Hop-scotch. Look how wide the windowsills are, you could almost sleep on them."

"You wouldn't have to," said Jean hastily. "The bedrooms are upstairs. Come see."

"Are the stairs safe?"

"Of course," said Jean, and Donald stamped his foot on one to prove it.

The empty wallpapered bedrooms stood waiting.

"Only two?" said Mrs. Monroe. "I suppose they bundled all the children in together."

"There's a huge attic," said Donald.

She followed them up the narrow stairs, and crouched down at the window to admire the view, and bumped her head on a rafter standing up, just as Jean had done.

"Now the kitchen," said Jean.

They took her back downstairs. Jean inspected her face in the soft gray light, trying to see what she thought, but she seemed only a little baffled, waiting for something more.

Donald demonstrated the pump at the sink, and made her try the water.

"It's delicious," she said. "I suppose it's a well." She wiped her mouth on her sleeve and looked at her waiting children. "So?" she said. "Where is it? The surprise you had?"

Donald looked at Jean. She took a deep breath. It seemed silly again, like the horse show, and she could feel her face getting red.

Mrs. Monroe smiled and frowned, waiting.

"We cleaned it up," she stammered desperately.

"That's nice."

"Not to be nice. Because . . . because, Mother, we want to live here. You, too, I mean."

"*Live* here?"

Mrs. Monroe's waiting, frowning face broke up, and she leaned on the drainboard and laughed and laughed. "Oh, Jeannie, Jeannie, my raving mad lamb," she gasped. "What am I going to do with you?"

"I don't see what's so funny," said Donald staunchly.

"There isn't any plumbing, you nut. This is an *old* house, an old deserted house. They've got an outhouse in the back, a privy. Didn't you see it? There's no bathroom. Do you know how much it costs to put in plumbing? A fortune, believe me."

"There's electricity," Jean mumbled miserably. She hated

her mother with a great choking, strangling wave of hate. She could say no, but how could she laugh? How could she?

"Electricity isn't plumbing."

"Millions of people live without plumbing," said Donald.

"For all I know, millions of people may live on Mars," said Mrs. Monroe. "No, lambs, it's ridiculous. But look, if you're sure it's all right with Mrs. Remington, you could certainly come here to play."

"Play," cried Jean.

"You could have it for a sort of clubhouse. Maybe you could even camp here next summer. Bring your sleeping bags."

"It'll be a shopping center next summer," said Donald.

"Then we couldn't live here anyway, could we?"

"The rent money," said Donald. "If we paid her rent, Mrs. Remington, then she could pay the taxes. Then she wouldn't have to sell it to . . . oh, never mind. Forget I mentioned it." He worked the pump handle up and down and watched the water guggle down the drain to the lilies outside.

Jean turned blindly away to hide her face, and opened a cupboard door and stared in, blinking, at the empty, scrubbed shelves. She was suddenly absolutely exhausted, and held on to the cupboard door to keep from collapsing and slumping down onto the yellow linoleum.

There was nothing more she could do. She had tried and tried, and nothing was any use.

"I'm sorry you went to so much trouble," said Mrs. Monroe. "It must have been a lot of work. But, really, my lambs, you should have known better."

"It was Jean's idea," said Donald. "But I don't see what's so crazy about it."

"You *don't*?"

"No," said Donald, with spirit. "I don't. We'd do all the extra work, it wouldn't be that hard. We'd get used to it, easier than getting used to Mrs. Pike, or Mr. Wilcox. We'd have a hot bath waiting for you every day when you got home from work, if you wanted."

"Bath? Where?"

"Here, in the kitchen. You know those tub things they had, sort of pear-shaped?"

"I've seen pictures. They don't make them any more. Needless to say."

"There's one up in the barn, in the loft. I saw it."

"And what about our poor delicate old car? Where would it live?"

"Plenty of room in the barn."

"Oh, Donald, be reasonable. I thought you were my *sane* child. What about laundry, what about going out back to the privy, in the rain, and wintertime?"

Jean said, bitterly, into the depths of the cupboard, "Didn't you ever hear of chamber pots? Or laundromats?"

Mrs. Monroe put her hands on her hips and said, "Now, listen. Both of you."

At that point the front door groaned and a small voice called, "Hello? Are you here? I saw the car."

"In the kitchen," said Donald.

Mrs. Remington appeared, carrying a bottle and the two smudgy glasses. "I just wondered," she said apologetically, "whether you'd like a little glass of sherry, for the cold."

"I certainly would," said Mrs. Monroe.

Mrs. Remington poured it out, her hand shaking, and spilled some on the drainboard. "I suppose these children have been telling you about their wild notion?"

"Yes," said Mrs. Monroe. "Thank you." She tasted the sherry. "I'm sorry if they've been a nuisance to you."

"Why, no. Actually it's been very pleasant to have them

around. I don't see many people, you know. Cheers."

"Cheers. Just don't let my Jeannie talk you into anything," said Mrs. Monroe. "She tends to get ideas. She can't stop herself. Like. . . ." She waved her hand around at the kitchen, and the house.

Mrs. Remington nodded. "Out of the question, of course." She fiddled with the knobs on the kitchen stove. Nothing happened. "No gas. Runs on bottled gas, you know. Gracious, I haven't been in here for years. Not since . . . I can't remember." Her bright blue eyes looked off into nothing, searching for the memory like a sailor looking for land. "Mr. Hagerty, was that his name? All those children. Five or six of them. Their Billy, my, he was a hellion. Fell out of the cherry tree and broke his leg. Or his arm, perhaps. Used to ride the cow. We had a cow in those days. Everyone did, of course."

"Six children?" said Mrs. Monroe. *"Here?"*

"Perhaps it was only five. It seemed like six. More sherry? A perfectly absurd idea, as I told these two. No plumbing. All that work."

"It isn't the work, so much," said Mrs. Monroe, perching on the edge of the wobbly kitchen table. "The children have always been good about that."

"The outhouse. 'Necessary house,' they used to call it. Dreadfully inconvenient."

"Chamber pots," said Jean again, and went to stand in the open doorway and look out, past the old lilac to the rising slope of the field, dotted with ponies. Now that it was over, she only wanted to get away, as far away as she could, just run and keep on running forever.

"Ah, chamber pots," said Mrs. Remington fondly. "I've got a whole collection of them somewhere. Valuable antiques, I suppose they are now. And then there's the ghost."

"Really?" Mrs. Monroe raised her eyebrows.

"Ghost?" said Donald. "How neat."

"Oh, gracious, it's no one important. The officers were quartered in the big house. This fellow was just an aide-de-camp or some such. Walks around once in a while, up in the attic. The Hagertys complained. And then, of course, the isolation." Mrs. Remington sipped her sherry and looked out the window. There wasn't a house in sight. "No neighbors. To tell you the truth, one tends to get a bit *odd* with no neighbors to keep one in line."

Mrs. Monroe went to stand beside her and look out. "I'm afraid the Monroes are a bit odd already. At least, *our* neighbors think so . . . I wonder how that Mrs. Hagerty managed. With all those kids, and no plumbing."

"Oh, people didn't mind then. Seemed more natural to them, back before the war. Didn't wash as much, I expect, and used to it all. But for people like you, of course. . . ."

"Yes," said Mrs. Monroe absently. "And no neighbors, you said? No neighbors at all? Where *is* the nearest house?"

"Down the lane. The Burdetts. Crusty old fellow, never speaks. Yard full of trash."

The sun struggled briefly through a gap in the clouds and a thin splash of light struck through the window. Outside, leaves swirled on the ground, and Hopscotch came to the honeysuckle fence and whinnied toward the house.

Mrs. Monroe turned away from the window. "I think," she said, "I would like to look around again, if it's all right. I'd like to see upstairs again. Now, kids, don't look at me like that. All I said was I'd like to see upstairs."

"I'll come with you," said Mrs. Remington. "Treacherous stairs, as I remember."

Donald and Jean faced each other across the kitchen table. They could hear Mrs. Remington puffing on the steps, and then feet on the bare floors overhead. Donald chewed the edge of his thumbnail.

"Donald," hissed Jean.

"Shut up," he said. "Just kindly shut up."

A rusty, crunching noise came from the other room, and Mrs. Remington's voice floated down to them, saying, "to heat the bedrooms, you know. Open the gratings here in the floor, and the heat from the wood stove comes up from the living room. Very primitive, I'm afraid."

"Oh, *damn,* I can't stand it," said Jean. She ran out through the kitchen door, and across the chopped weeds to the fence to throw her arms around Hopscotch and hide her face in her neck. Her knees were quivering. "You need brushing," she muttered shakily into the fur. "You haven't been properly brushed in a week."

After a long time, Mrs. Monroe and Mrs. Remington came out of the little house, Mrs. Remington carrying the sherry bottle. They walked up the long drive slowly, talking, were greeted by a shouting of dogs, and disappeared into the big house.

Jean clambered over the fence and pulled herself up onto Hopscotch's warm back. The pony moved along the fence-row, cropping the brown grass. One of the grays, the one Jean was calling Stormy, came to nose jealously at her leg.

Presently the dogs barked again, and Jean watched the two women come out of the big house and go into the barn.

Jean sat on Hopscotch, her fingers nervously jerking burrs out of the blond mane as if they had minds of their own.

Swallows darted and swirled around the hole in the barn roof. When the bulldozers come, Jean thought, they can push the whole barn right down the hill into the stream. The big house too, and then cover everything up by pushing the top of the hill down over them. They wouldn't have to carry anything away. Then it would all be flat and ready for

114

paving, ready for a long row of little stores and one big department store.

The picture got confused, and she could see ponies in the parking lot, Hopscotch and the others. Terrified by the cars, they would run wildly back and forth, slipping on the black asphalt, wheeling frantically. Horns would blow, and people wind down their windows and yell. The ponies would dash slithering over their old pasture, but there'd be no place to go, no grass, just angry people and horns blowing. No corner left where a pony could live.

She bent over to wipe her eyes on Hopscotch's mane, and when she straightened up the women had come back out of the barn, her tall mother and stumpy Mrs. Remington, and started down the long maple drive. They were carrying things.

Jean squinched her eyes up tightly to see. Mrs. Remington was carrying or dragging something as tall as she was, something pear-shaped that looked like a mummy case, exactly like a mummy case.

She tried to urge Hopscotch closer to the fence, but the pony, bridleless, paid no attention and went on eating weeds.

Her mother was carrying two round things like big bowls, or basins. They came closer. They seemed to be laughing. Her mother's walk looked loose and happy, and she swung one of the round things by its rim. It was white, with something on it, something pink, like painted roses.

As they turned toward the little house, Mrs. Monroe looked over and saw Jean, and laughed out loud and held it up to show her. Yes, there were roses painted on it.

It was a chamber pot, and the mummy case was the tub.

They were carrying the bathroom for the little stone house.

14

"You can have this," said Jean. "And this too, if you want it. And you can have all my plastic horses."

"You mean it?" asked Shelley. "Even the little gray with the saddle?"

Jean held it a minute in her hand. It stood, as always, at a prance, one tiny hoof curled up, its neck arched. It felt cool and smooth, most unhorse-like, but she had ridden it miles and miles in her mind, before Hopscotch. She kissed its head and handed it to Shelley. Shelley, she thought, really liked plastic horses better than real ones.

"Thanks. I'll take good care of it."

"I'm going to have plenty of real horses. Mrs. Remington said I could work with her ponies, not the little bay that's foundered, but the others. I thought I'd retrain them, maybe. You could come over and help me, and we could give riding lessons when we get them in shape. If we made some money, we could use it to start a kind of place where people could bring horses that were old, or nobody wanted or didn't have a place for, like Hopscotch. So they wouldn't have to be put to sleep."

"I'll come over," said Shelley. "I don't know if I could help or anything."

"Okay, you can just ride Hopscotch, then."

"I can't believe you're really leaving," said Shelley. "And Jean? Listen, I'm sorry about that stuff I said. About the horse show. You know."

"Well, you were right, anyway," said Jean cheerfully.

"Sort of. But just about the show. Because look, you did save Highmeadow, didn't you? And you got the house you wanted. I guess maybe for people like you, things like that aren't so weird. Sometimes you can, like, do things."

"Anybody can," said Jean, from under the bed where she was rummaging in socks and books.

"Not me," said Shelley firmly, and with satisfaction. "I'm not like that. But it's okay for you, I guess."

"Oh, Shelley!" Jean came out, red in the face, with her hat knocked crooked. "It's going to be so *great*. Living there. Wait till you see it."

"With no bathroom."

"How many people do you know with no bathroom?" demanded Jean triumphantly.

"Just you. Nobody else would think of it even for a minute, even for a second. Listen, I've got to go. I told Mom I'd be right back. Thanks for the horses."

And for the last time Shelley's feet clattered down the stairs.

Alone, Jean dumped another pile of clothes and a drawerful of papers from her desk into a carton, and marked it with crayon, WEST BEDROOM, and went to the bathroom for her toothbrush.

Tomorrow, she thought, no, tonight, I will pump a glass of water and brush my teeth at the kitchen sink. Good-bye, bathroom.

117

Good-bye, Mrs. Wilcox, Mr. Reece, Mrs. Pike.

If I come back someday, she thought, to look for this house again, I probably won't be able to find it. The new people will plant grass on the patch where Hopscotch lived, and put in a new azalea bush where the dead one is, and it'll look just like all the others. I could come back, and stand and look at a house and think, that's where I used to live, there's my bedroom window, and I'd be looking at the wrong house. The Reeces', or the Simmers'.

Silly. There was always the number, 10007 Maryellen Lane.

The new house had no number. Their new address was Highmeadow, Washingtons Road.

In the medicine-cabinet mirror she straightened her hat, and then, first closing the bathroom door, she took it off and leaned close to the mirror to look. She picked some flaxen Hopscotch hairs from her brush, and brushed experimentally at her head.

Underneath the rusty-looking greenish-black, really lots of her own hair had come back in. She could get the awful part cut off. What was left would be short, very short indeed, but her own, at least. She wouldn't have to wear the hat any more. She wouldn't need it.

If you were the only girl in school who lived in an old stone house with a ghost and no plumbing and seven ponies outside, you didn't need to be the only girl with blackish-green hair under a man's hunting hat.

As soon as they were settled, she'd ask her mother to take her into Bedlington for a haircut.

"Jean?" said Donald, through the bathroom door. "You want me to carry anything over? I'm going over now, on my bike, get the wood stove started so the place'll be warm. And ask the ghost if it plays chess."

She shoved the hat back on and opened the door. "There's my plant," she said. "I'm taking the gerbils in the car, but can you carry my orange plant in your basket?"

"I guess so. Poor thing, you ought to put it out of its misery."

She had started it from an orange seed, with some idea of growing bushels of their very own orange juice. It was always sickly and struggling, but it never quite died. Donald took it disapprovingly.

"I told you oranges won't grow in New Jersey," he said. "But wait till you see my tomatoes next summer. You can drink tomato juice instead."

"I never knew you were so outdoorsy," said Jean. "Who ever heard of a chess player growing tomatoes?"

"Actually, gardening's relaxing to the brain. It'll probably improve my game. And my math. You see, child, you take a really powerful brain, which you wouldn't know anything about, a genius, really, and it needs a certain amount of relaxation, like tomatoes. The mental strain—"

"Oh, shut up. Listen. Do you think you could relax your brain fixing up the barn? Because I was thinking, if we got the barn in shape, cleaned out the junk, and we put some glass in the windows and fixed the door, and I got Mrs. Remington's ponies into condition, we could have a riding stable. Maybe if—"

"No!" said Donald. "You're going to have plenty to do, and so am I, emptying chamber pots and heating water and stuff. Just because we cleaned the house up a little, don't go thinking we're a whole construction company."

"But it wouldn't be that much—"

"No!" He turned and ran down the stairs, fluttering the poor orange plant and shouting, "No, and no, and NO!" The front door banged.

Jean got another box and went on with her packing. Maybe she could do it herself. She'd have to get someone with a truck to carry the junk away. But how do you put glass in windows? Just stick it on, with tape or something? She inspected the window of her bedroom. Was the glass *inside* the little frame pieces, like a sandwich?

Outside the window, Mrs. Reece was pushing the stroller very slowly along the sidewalk, staring at the Monroes'. Hoping they were leaving soon. Hoping the new people would come, and plant grass, and not keep ponies. The new people they had finally found to buy the house, new people who loved it, a woman who was crazy about stupid things like the oven, and the laundry room, empty now of ponies. Mrs. Reece would like her.

Good-bye, Mrs. Reece.

The sky looked like snow. Soft and heavy and gray, smelling damp. Maybe it would snow for Christmas. Christmas was soon. Christmas in the new house, with the little wood stove roaring cheerily, and white fields stretching away out the window. Ponies galloping, kicking up sprays of snow, snorting steam. A gallop across the field before school in the morning, with Hopscotch bucking for joy in the cold air.

Goodness, she thought suddenly, I own a pony. I actually won that pony in the contest, and she's my very own forever. It's been such a fuss and problem that I never had time to realize. *I have a pony.* Wow.

Here on Maryellen Lane, Christmas would come without them. They wouldn't see the life-size Santa Claus and sleigh and plastic reindeer on the Pikes' front lawn this year, or hear the Wilcoxes' loudspeaker thing that played "Rudolph the Red-Nosed Reindeer" every night for three weeks.

They would see snow and ponies, and maybe Mrs. Remington would put candles in her windows for Christmas. She looked like a person who put candles in her windows. The Monroes would see them, just barely, up the long drive, through their long windows that wouldn't have curtains in them because the old curtains were too short and too wide. If you didn't have neighbors, you didn't need curtains.

Her mother came in, looking distracted. "What are you mooning out the window for, Jean? Aren't you finished yet? What about your books, do you need another box? There're some more downstairs, but don't use the big ones for books. They're too heavy. The men'll be here in twenty minutes, or at least they said they would."

"I'm hurrying, I'm hurrying. No, I've got boxes." She pulled a stack of books from her bookcase and dumped them in on top of her sweaters.

"I still can't believe it," said her mother, and giggled nervously. "I still feel as if there must be *some* reason we can't do it. It has to be impossible, but I just can't think why."

"There isn't any reason," said Jean firmly. "Move, you're standing on my bathrobe."

"I suppose it's an adventure. I guess that's why I feel so peculiar. Maybe people don't have enough adventures any more, maybe it's good for them." She giggled again. "No plumbing, dear heavenly saints. A chamber pot covered with hand-painted roses. Baths in the kitchen."

"You'll get used to it," Jean promised. "You won't even think it's an adventure, it'll just feel usual."

"Well, just don't give me any *more* adventures. This one's enough for a while."

Jean decided it was the wrong time to mention the riding stable idea, or ask about getting a cow.

"Finish," said her mother, pointing sternly to the bookcase, and went downstairs singing "Over the Sea to Skye."

Jean finished taking apart and packing up the room she had lived in for two years. On the shelf in the closet she found a white sock and an Easter basket full of dusty sea shells and the bald china doll's head from the fallen-down house on the hill.

She threw the sock and the shells in the trash bag, and started to toss the doll's head after them, but it stared up at her with its mad blue eyes so intently that she stuffed it in her pocket instead.

Maybe it was magic, or lucky. Maybe Mrs. Remington was right about luck. She kept talking about it now, and how it was Jean who brought it back to Highmeadow, because of the shopping center people not getting it, and having to buy land clear down on the other side of Route 9, miles from where they wanted to be.

And of course, she *was* lucky. Nobody could possibly be luckier. But you couldn't go around leaning on luck too hard, not when there were so many things you could do to help it along, so many things you could do yourself, without it. Still, it was probably a good thing to have around, just in case. She would keep the doll's head.

"Jean!" called her mother. "They're here! The moving men are here, I see the truck!"

Jean threw a last quick look over her shoulder, grabbed up the gerbil cage, and pounded down the stairs for the last time, holding her hat with one hand, calling, "I'm ready! I'm coming!"